ENCOUNTER BY DEADLINE

Other books by Mel Taylor:

Murder by Deadline

ENCOUNTER BY DEADLINE

•

Mel Taylor

AVALON BOOKS
NEW YORK

Library of Congress Cataloging-in-Publication Data

Taylor, Mel.
    Encounter by deadline / Mel Taylor.
        p. cm.
    ISBN 978-0-8034-9839-6 (acid-free paper) 1. Television
journalists—Fiction. 2. Fort Lauderdale (Fla.)—Fiction.
I. Title.

PS3570.A9462E53 2007
813'.6—dc22

2007004990

PRINTED IN THE UNITED STATES OF AMERICA
ON ACID-FREE PAPER
BY HADDON CRAFTSMEN, BLOOMSBURG, PENNSYLVANIA

Dedicated to my brother, Steven,
and my sisters, Pat and Debbie

I want to thank the very talented members of the Thursday Group. Their support and input on the book meant a great deal. And I want to thank Joyce Sweeney, who started the group and continues to be a fantastic teacher, friend, and motivator.

I also got a great deal of help researching diamonds and the geographical makeup of beautiful south Florida.

Finally, I'd like to thank my family: Joyce, Karlynne, and Chris.

Chapter 1

I eased the briefcase next to the trash bin under my desk and circled Friday the eighth on the desk calendar. The calm of 7:30 in the morning never lasted past nine. PR firms, police agencies, and rip-off victims would be calling. Once a month, an anxious tenant detailed problems with a landlord.

On my right, a huge window opened up a view to the Intracoastal waterway. The Florida sun pushed darkness to the side, exposing Fort Lauderdale to the light. South Beach club-hoppers drifted back north across the county line, into the city for breakfast. Weary-eyed tourists, taxicab drivers, and truckers blended with rush hour traffic.

The newsroom was quiet. Columns of sunlight bleached areas on the floor near my desk. A mile out on the water, the ripples were flat and gray-blue, perfect conditions for fishing. Layers of clouds, seared in red tinges, blocked the full bore of the sunrise.

I heard the lock rattle, and the front door opened. Mike Brendon backed in, carrying a large box.

"Need some help?" I offered.

1

"No thanks, Matt." Brendon guided the box to a spot behind the assignment desk. He used his hand to smear the glaze from his forehead and adjusted his glasses. "The engineering department made me bring this up. They'll install it in a few days."

"What is it?"

Brendon swiped his brow again before he answered.

"It's the base for a new camera. They're installing it on our roof. Miami wants to use the camera for weather bump shots during the day and security at night."

"Just a reminder, Mike; I'm off on Friday," I told him. Brendon stroked the length of his crimson beard. The hint of a smile receded into the strands of a mustache. He eased the bulk of his two-hundred-sixty pound body into a chair, booted up his computer and, when he looked at me through smeared glasses, the half smile was back. "No Matt Bowens? You leaving town?"

I didn't know how to answer him. The last time I gave him my travel plans, he figured out where I booked my hotel room and he yanked me off vacation to cover a train derailment.

"We're just headed along the coast. No deadlines and no cell phones." I wasn't specific, and Brendon left it alone.

"I might be gone for a few minutes this afternoon," he told me. "My sugar levels are way off. Could be a fluke." Brendon was talking to the computer screen. He reached into his briefcase and took out a package, pulling back the crisp paper from a thick egg and bacon sandwich. Melted cheese dripped down one side of the bread. "My doctor doesn't like what he sees. Wants more tests." He set the sandwich to one side.

Brendon was the best TV news assignment editor in the

two-county area. He was reachable at home; every police and fire department kept him among their first contacts. One time, during full-tilt hurricane coverage, Mike stayed on the assignment desk, calmly sending reporters out. But he never left the desk. Over a two-day period, he ate and slept in front of his computer. The news director ordered him home once the storm missed us and headed north. Still, I was worried about his health.

The phone rang. Brendon jammed the receiver into the crook of his neck, while guiding a newspaper from the plastic wrapper, crushing the wrap into a nice ball. "Channel 14 News," he said. Brendon listened, aimed at a trash can and tossed the wrapper, basketball-style. All net.

Brendon said, "Can't take it. We're on a budget freeze. Can't buy any stringer video." He eased the phone down and started dialing.

The doorbell chimed. Brendon was busy on the phone, making morning checks with police departments. I opened the door to a woman checking her watch.

"Matt? I haven't seen you in what, a year? You have a minute?"

"Morgan?"

"Busy yet?" She said, looking around the newsroom.

"No. How's Cole?"

"That's what I want to talk to you about."

I directed Morgan Walker to a chair near the window and the yellow wall-sized Channel 14 logo. Her hair was pulled close to the scalp and tied in a loose bun in the back. If she shook her head even gently, the curls would fall to her shoulders. Age didn't show in her face until you noticed the puffiness under her green eyes.

"What's wrong?" I asked.

"You and Cole worked together for a long time." Her words were drawn out and deliberate.

"Ten years," I said.

"He always respected you as a reporter . . ."

"Thank you, but how is Cole?"

She pressed her fingers into her eyes and dragged her hands down the length of her face, pulling a single tear down the slope of a cheek, finally revealing a quiver of movement in her lips. She flicked her eyes, going from me to the purse on the floor.

"I haven't had any sleep. Cole didn't come home last night."

Mike Brendon stood up from his chair, telephone cords dangling from his head, a receiver pushed to each ear. "I could use some help on the phones," he yelled.

"In a second," I said, turning back to Morgan. "Does Cole normally check in with you?"

"Once every few hours, he'll give me a call. Always. A few times, he stayed out all night on stories, but he made sure to call. But last night, nothing after nine. I tried his cell, his pager, everything. He's been acting weird lately."

"Weird?"

"He's been getting calls late at night, and speaking so low I can't make out what he's saying."

"Any unusual clients?"

"Matt, Cole is a stringer. And your station is like everywhere else. They're cutting back on freelance photographers. Cole has been taking on several different clients instead of news stations. He won't tell me what he's been working on. I shouldn't be worried, but I am."

I remembered Cole taking Morgan to Friday-night gatherings where reporters and photographers stopped for beer and wine at La Luna Lounge. We exchanged stories of covering street crime and promised to meet again. After that, I saw Morgan the day Cole Walker put down his camera.

The day changed him forever.

Cole arrived first before the paramedics, to see a gunshot victim sprawled on the lawn. Two shots to the face. Another in the neck. All close range. Cole found himself alone with a stranger. A crimson pool gathered near the man's head, seeping into the grass. Cole bent down next to him. The victim tried to speak, mouthing gasps of words Cole couldn't understand. Air in the form of blood bubbles escaped from the gape in his neck. He stopped talking. And then he was gone. His eyes remained open, locked in death until they were closed later by the medical examiner. Cole watched a man die. Without taking a single frame of video, Cole Walker put his camera on the ground, vowing to never pick it up again.

Cole quit his job that night. He left his camera gear in the newsroom, and Morgan came to pick him up. I made him come to a good-bye gathering. Five months later, Cole told me, after working through the nightmares, it was Morgan who convinced him to start working again as a stringer; a hired freelance photographer, paid by the news story for any station eager to spend the bucks. I had no contact with Morgan. Until now.

"Did Cole say where he was going last night?"

"No."

"Does he keep a work order, invoice, anything to say where he might be working?"

"I checked his desk. Nothing. But a few days ago, he insisted he had to call you. That's the reason I'm here. I thought maybe he told you something."

"He say why?"

"He just pointed to the wall of videotapes we have." Morgan rolled her eyes at the ceiling.

"Any tape in particular?"

She reached down and separated the folds in her purse. "I'm guessing this one. If it's okay, I want to see the tape. Now."

Morgan pulled out an unmarked videotape case. "You should have seen his face when I touched it one day, in his 'so called' hiding place. Cole exploded on me . . . told me never to go near it again."

"This tape? And you think—"

"I don't think anything. It's just that I haven't heard from him all night and I'm reaching."

She handed me the tape box, opening the gray case in the process. Two sparkling objects fell and rolled toward a worn spot in the carpet. We stayed transfixed on their shape and radiance. Each orb glittered with the roll as though they gave off sparks. We sat in silence, staring at the luster of two thimble-sized diamonds.

Chapter 2

Morgan Walker gathered the diamonds off the floor and held one up to the morning light. "I've never seen these before."

"You didn't open up the case?" I asked.

"No. I thought it was just a tape."

She turned her attention to the diamond. The large gem reflected sun darts on her cheeks. Mike Brendon was standing at our back, no longer on the assignment desk. "Who won the lottery?" His eyes were locked on the dazzle in Morgan's fingers. "Where did they come from?"

"We're not sure," I said, taking a diamond from her hand. "What is this, eight carats?"

"A lot larger I think." She lowered her hand. The gleam died in Morgan's gaze. "That still doesn't tell me about Cole."

I showed Brendon the videotape case. The tape was still inside the box. "They must have been jammed inside here." I pointed to the circular gaps in the two tape spools, room enough to hide something small.

Morgan dropped back into the chair. I pulled Brendon

aside and explained her concerns about Cole. He moved back behind the desk and picked up the phone.

"Mike is going to check the hospitals and cop shops. Maybe someone heard something. You want to hold on to these?" I studied the shimmer, letting the diamond roll around in my palm so the facets could burn with their own brilliance, finally dropping the gem back into her hand.

"And Cole never mentioned he had these?"

"Not a word."

"I can probably guess, but how many tape boxes does Cole have at the house?"

"Hundreds."

The front door opened and photographer Ike Cashing stepped into the room. His face took on a curious look. Cashing was thin, his khaki pants drooped a bit over a worn pair of running shoes. A green polo shirt, embroidered with a Channel 14 logo, was wrinkled.

"Hello, Morgan," he said.

Morgan dipped her head toward the floor and used her hand to smooth a few wild strands back into place. Cashing stepped past the arrangement of desks toward Morgan. He stopped as she lifted her head.

"Cole Walker didn't make it home last night," I told him. "You catch anything on your scanner? Maybe he's still working on something?"

"There's a truck rollover in Miami, but I doubt he'd travel that far from the Fort Lauderdale area. The helicopters usually take in all that video." As he spoke, Ike kept shaking his head, staring in the direction of the diamonds.

"I don't think Mike has us assigned yet," I said. "Do you want to take a ride somewhere and look for Cole?"

"I wouldn't know where to start." Morgan glanced at the box in my hand.

"Can you load this tape first? We'd like to take a look." I gave Ike the videotape. We followed him to the first edit booth. He flipped buttons, turned on machines, and adjusted volumes, then inserted the tape into the playdeck. In seconds, a picture filled the screens of two television monitors. The video showed the mayor of Fort Lauderdale, mouth open, frozen in mid-sentence until Ike hit the play button. I turned up the volume. We listened to the mayor talk about future city plans.

"I remember this," I said. "It's the state of the city address." We watched the tape for the next few minutes. Ike, obviously bored with hearing about future building plans, put the tape in the forward search mode and pinched his eyes shut, letting a hard yawn spasm through his body. He dug a finger at the sleep in his eyes. "Can you tell me what we're looking for?"

"We don't know yet ourselves," I said. "I just want to look at the entire tape."

"No problem." Ike took the player out of search and let the tape play. The mayor talked about construction projects, clean parks, and tourist-laden beaches, until applause ended the speech.

"There's nothing here." I spoke to the television monitors.

"You try calling Cole again?" Ike looked into Morgan's stare. She held the diamonds in her closed fist.

"I called him just before I came here. No answer. But I can try again." She backed out of the booth, taking small steps until she stopped by the window.

"What's this about?" Ike whispered. "Where did those diamonds come from?"

"Not now."

"Are they having problems? I bet he's holed up some-where."

"And maybe not," I said.

Ike called it playing the sides. After murder scenes or high stakes robberies, he offered his hunches. By the time the uniforms pulled down the crime tape, after we recorded our interviews, Ike figured out a suspect and mo-tive. Most of the time, his predictions were valid.

The lines in Ike's forehead bunched up and he kept his voice low. "Maybe he's seeing someone on the side."

I ignored Ike and studied Morgan. She used her index finger to pick at the diamonds, as if they might give her a clue on where to find Cole.

Ike handed me the tape. I slid the tape inside the box, left the edit room, and handed the box to Morgan.

"Have you looked through any files on your computer at home?" I asked.

"Cole never uses the computer. I do." I followed Mor-gan's stare to some envelopes sticking out of a stack of papers on my desk.

"Can I have one?" She asked.

I pulled out an envelope. Her hand trembled as she dropped the diamonds inside and stuck the envelope in her purse.

"Those are *some* diamonds," Ike said. He got a look on his face as though he wanted to grab his camera. He stepped closer to Morgan.

"No," she whispered, rolling her eyes at the ceiling. "I should have called work."

"Don't worry about that. Give me the number and I'll give them a call." She handed me a business card.

"C'mon, Matt, what's the deal on the diamonds?" The eyebrows in Ike's face kicked upward.

"Right now our main concern is finding Cole. I'll tell you later about the diamonds."

Morgan glanced at us briefly, then turned again to the window.

"Guess the only thing I can do now is go home and wait," she sighed. Her eyes appeared weak. She rested her hands on the window sill and stared at the boat slips. It was late January in Fort Lauderdale. The place was bustling with winter visitors from around the world. I didn't interrupt Morgan's silent watch of the brackish water. A pelican floated at a slow pace, heavy and long-billed, gliding over the boats tied down in the soft buffet of winds blowing through the marina.

I imagined Morgan the way she looked one night at La Luna Lounge. Fingers snapping to the beat, she jerked Cole out of his chair, urging him to a scratched parquet floor, while patrons tapped their feet to the thump of the music. Twice Cole tried to sit down rather than dance, but Morgan pulled him into a steady pace of gyrations. No one else ventured onto the floor, preferring instead to watch Cole's beer-induced collection of foot slides and hip thrusts. She kept him out there for three songs. When they finished, Morgan's shoulders glistened with sweat, and Cole asked for another round. A wave of guilt swept through me for not keeping in touch with him since he left the station.

When Morgan turned away from the window, she looked smaller somehow, as though the search for Cole was consuming her, breaking her down, folding in her shoulders, from the sheer weight of not knowing.

"Morgan." Mike's voice carried a certain authority. Her head turned in the direction of Mike's voice.

"I just confirmed it with the fire-rescue. They've got someone in emergency. A John Doe. No I.D., but the description sounds like Cole."

"Did they say what happened?" Morgan licked the cracked lines etched in her bottom lip. Brendon stood, making eye contact with me rather than Morgan. She moved a step closer to him as if to get his attention. "Mike. Tell me what they said."

"They told me it was a gunshot victim."

Chapter 3

"Y ou'll have to stay here." The nurse pointed me to a chair in a small waiting room of Fort Lauderdale Metro General Hospital.

"Only family members are allowed in the ICU." The nurse gave no hint of a smile until she touched Morgan's arm, leading her to a wide hallway and past a sign marked INTENSIVE CARE UNIT. Ike stayed downstairs in the lobby.

"I'll let you know something," Morgan said over her shoulder. She walked slower than the nurse and had to double-step to match the pace. I watched Morgan and the nurse until they turned a corner and stepped out of view.

The hospital walls had the same somber gray hue of a January Chicago sky. It was years removed, but I was left with the jagged images of that day; the chipped brown brick of the housing project, graffiti-tagged walls and the faces without hope, standing on the street corner holding half bottles of gutter cheap wine. I zipped up my jacket to keep out the chilled air blowing off Lake Michigan.

A gun barrel protruded from the back window of a passing car as I stepped from the curb. I was close enough to see his hands tightening on the grip and taking aim, his wintry breath, shouting, "Die!"

Muzzle blast echoed against the ice-streaked car windows.

I felt myself falling.

My body picked up speed, drifting to the sidewalk, easy as a heavy Chicago snowfall. My right arm jerked outward instinctively, palm and fingers flat against the wind as if to stop a bullet, like a plea might prevent another black kid from being shot down in the street.

I awoke to lines of IV's. I tried to move but the pain rippled through my body somewhere under the layers of bandages across my chest. Groggy, I eased my head back and let my mind assess what happened. My mouth was dry, and my lips felt swollen. I heard movement and focused on a corner of the room. I gazed upward into the smile of a nurse approaching my bed. There were voices in the room. Someone bellowed about black-on-black crime and would police be motivated to find the shooter.

A finger touched my shoulder once, then tapped harder and I was no longer in Chicago. The image died.

"I'm sorry, I forgot your name, and I don't watch television." The nurse seemed impatient for an answer.

"Matt Bowens."

"They told me you're a TV reporter, not immediate family. You okay? You seem—"

"I'm fine." I ran my fingers across my starched shirt, where I could still feel the hard surface of the scar where the bullet hit my chest, just to the left of my heart.

"Is Morgan back?" I stood up, in a way of showing I was prepared to follow the nurse to Morgan.

"She's with a detective right now. She identified her

husband. I'm sorry but you're going to have to wait downstairs."

"How is Cole?"

Her brow lines converged. "I'm afraid I can't say a lot because of confidentiality, all those new guidelines, you understand. But I'll let her know you want to speak to her."

"Morgan wouldn't mind if you told me how he's doing. He's a friend."

"I'm sorry. I can't say anything."

The elevator door opened and several chairs in the hospital lobby were occupied by a reporter or photographer. Sandra Capers pushed up from her seat, a pad by her side. When she saw it was me, her face appeared anxious.

"Where are you coming from?" She thumped the pad against her leg with the cadence of someone who demanded an answer.

"Sandra." I walked past her, ignoring her question, finally settling into the worn depression of a tattered chair. The hard steps of heels on the hospital floor echoed in my direction until Capers stopped a few feet from me.

Capers said, "We're not allowed up there. You got anything going, Bowens?"

"Look, I can't get into it right now. Call the hospital marketing people. They'll probably tell you everything I know."

Capers let a smile form across her face, but her eyes were still locked in a glare. She shifted her writing pad from her side to a position in front of her, fingers pushing around the edges of the pad.

"It's okay." Capers stepped away from me and toward her photographer. He almost dropped a Channel 8 microphone, finally catching the mike as he moved it from his hand to a mount on top of the camera.

Minutes later a security guard approached me. "Excuse me, but the reporter over there is accusing you of sneaking upstairs to get information." He cocked his head toward Capers.

I said, "You can check with the nursing staff. I didn't sneak into the hospital. I came with a friend. Her husband has been shot. When they told me to leave the ICU, I did."

The guard stood there, taking in my words, probably weighing them with the charge from Capers. "She is demanding access to the waiting room upstairs, and we can't let her do that. You know the rules."

"I understand. I was up there for only a few minutes."

"But you don't have a hallway pass." His voice was controlled but firm. "Nowadays you can't go anywhere without a pass. How did you manage that?"

"Again, I repeat, I came in through emergency with a friend. Her name is Morgan Walker. I think you better get marketing on the phone and get them down here."

The guard turned his back to me, and reached for his radio. He said a few words, then paused. A garbled response on his radio came a few seconds later.

"Someone is coming downstairs," he said.

"Thanks."

I pulled out my cell phone and dialed Mike Brendon.

"Channel 14," Mike said.

"It's Matt."

Brendon said, "Two things. We got some video of Cole being transported into the emergency room. I broke down and spent the money on some stringer video. And second, Morgan is trying to reach you. She said to meet her in the parking lot, away from everyone. There's something she wants to tell you."

Chapter 4

Morgan brushed past a security guard near the entrance of the emergency room and searched the parking lot until her eyes locked on mine. Her hair was down, and the wind kept the curls from collecting against her back.

"He's still out," Morgan said. "They've got him hooked up to so many things." Her voice dropped to a whisper. "The doctors say he's lucky, but he lost a lot of blood."

"If you need anything, let me know."

"When he wakes up, a detective wants to talk to him."

"His name?"

"Victor. Detective Henry Victor. I have his card. I just don't know about Cole."

"They got him to the hospital; he's in good hands now." My words still didn't raise the confidence in her eyes. "Where did they find him?"

"In a warehouse district, near Broward Boulevard." Her face was directed at me, squared up, eyes weak. "Can you tell me what you find out? The detectives aren't telling me much. They ask all the questions but they're not good at answering mine."

"Who found him?"

"They won't even tell me that. I mean, I want to give someone a thank you."

"They're just protecting the case. They have to be a bit indifferent."

Morgan shifted her feet and blinked back a tear. Ike stood nearby holding the camera.

"They could be a bit more helpful. They keep treating me like I'm some kind of—"

"They're just doing their jobs. You know that. Did you tell them about the diamonds?"

"No." Morgan looked defensive. Her body turned just a bit. She pushed her purse to her back and away from my view.

"The police are going to want to know about the diamonds—"

"Matt, I know I showed them to you but I wasn't thinking it out. Maybe I should have waited?"

"You didn't know they were in the case. What if—"

"That's just it; we don't know what these diamonds mean, so why get the police involved?" Morgan's voice kicked up in volume. "I mean, since we don't know anything about where they came from, we could be getting Cole into some kind of trouble."

"And we could be pointing police toward the shooter."

"I can't do it, Matt. Not right now. That's why I need your help."

"Detective Victor can help you—"

"I'll help the detective in any way I can, but I'm not going to implicate Cole in anything. Cole wouldn't be mixed up in anything bad."

"I'm not saying that. I'm just saying let Victor in on this. He might be able to help sort it out."

I reasoned with my reporter instinct to just tell the facts about the diamonds. My reporter's gut feeling told me to put the diamonds in my story.

"You know this isn't right. I have to report it."

"Just a short wait. That's all." A gust of wind sorted through the heavy branches of the banyan tree behind her, moving a dappled pattern of sunspots across her face. But her eyes stayed transfixed on me.

"Just tell Detective Victor about the diamonds."

"I don't know," Morgan whispered. "I can't do it." She dropped her hands to her sides, easing her fingers off the purse. Her right hand came up to touch my arm. "Cole trusted you. He confided in you. Help me on this. Let's find out more first before we make it public."

By not giving up the diamonds, Morgan could be holding back key evidence. The cops might call it obstruction of justice. I weighed everything I knew about Cole. A clean record. No arrests. And when we worked together, there were no hints of a hidden past. Morgan pushed her hand through her hair, her eyes focused on me as if my answer would help or destroy Cole.

I said, "I've got to run this by the news director. If he says hold it, I will."

"Thank you. First, let me know what you find out from police," Morgan said. "I promise, anything I get, I'll share information with you. But I've got to solve this diamond thing without the police. For now. If we find out it has something to do with what happened, then of course, I'll give them up."

I reached for the microphone.

"Can we do an interview?"

Morgan nodded. I played with the top of my reporter pad, anxious to take down some notes.

Morgan stepped closer. "Tell you what—if I can't get a read on this by this afternoon, I'll share the information with Detective Victor and you. Diamonds and all. How's that?" Morgan glanced at her watch. "You ready? I've got to get back upstairs."

"Again, I'll run this by the news director."

Ike adjusted the camera on his shoulder, and aimed the lens at Morgan's face. I checked the wireless microphone to make sure it was in the on mode and raised it to her face.

"Does Cole have any enemies? Any idea who would do this?"

Morgan paused. "My husband never spoke about anyone who would harm him. He's up there in a hospital bed, and I just want to make a public plea to anyone who might have seen something. He was found in the warehouse district. Maybe someone driving by saw a car, or a person, or a license plate. On behalf of my husband, I am asking you to come forward and call police."

"Any idea why he was at the warehouse?"

"Cole doesn't always give me a list of places he photographs. He checks in at least twice during the night when he is shooting video. When he didn't check in, I got worried."

A look of uncertainty settled into Morgan's eyes. I heard the jostling of equipment behind me before I saw the face. I turned back. Sandra Capers was running full stride across the parking lot. Her photographer was two yards behind her. She reached us by the time I asked another question.

"What have the doctors told you?" I asked.

"Not much. They're doing a number of examinations. I have to see them later."

"But he was shot?" Sandra Capers used the last of her breath getting the question out. I heard her sucking in air as Morgan answered.

"He was shot once, yes."

"Sandra Capers, Channel 8." Capers stopped to take in another chest full of air. "Sorry, but we just ran around the building. I didn't know you were giving interviews."

"I have to get back upstairs." Morgan turned to leave.

Capers moved with her. "Just a question or two, please. Did police find anything at the scene? Drugs?"

Morgan's lips mashed into a thin sliver. "The only one mentioning drugs is you. And you should be very careful about getting into something that's not true. As far as I know, there was nothing like that found at the scene. My husband is a victim. I'm trying to do what I can to find out who singled him out."

Morgan stepped away from the cameras as Capers shouted another question. Morgan kept going.

Capers turned toward me. "Sneaking around isn't your style, Matt. Or is this the new Channel 14 way of getting an edge?" Capers lowered the microphone down by her side.

"No one is sneaking around. She called me."

Chapter 5

The Broward Boulevard warehouse district was a series of single-story buildings, each with large metal doors, which rolled up and away to reveal individual shops, a car-repair garage, cut-rate sofa sales, and a neighborhood hardware store. Together the cream stucco structures formed a giant U.

Once out of the car, the smells hit me. Plastic covers on new couches emanated from my left. Two stalls down someone was cutting wood and a plume of sawdust gathered just outside the opening. Six units down, trails of yellow crime tape stretched from a police car to a utility pole. The metal barrier was down, but a house door, installed to the far right side, allowed people to enter.

Two unmarked cars were parked next to the police van. A crime scene technician walked from the warehouse and into the sunshine. She pulled up her plastic gloves and looked around until she got the attention of a detective. The tech whispered something to him and they both moved inside.

I visualized them checking for blood, fingerprints, and

fiber. While the techs worked, the business of the stalls kept going. The saw continued to churn at a high pitch, cutting into wood.

"Can't give you much right now." The words were coming from Patrick O'Donnell, a black police officer with an Irish name.

"Anything you have, I'll take it." I pulled out my reporter pad and adjusted the pen. "And I mean anything."

"I'm sorry to hear about Cole."

"Thank you."

"We're talking to the guy who found him . . ." He paused and checked his own handwriting on a yellow legal pad. "Yeah, make that two witnesses. We're talking to the people who found Mr. Walker but they won't be available to you guys for awhile, if ever." O'Donnell let his eyes drift down his page of notes. "Ah, we got the call at six-fifteen A.M. Two employees for one of the businesses got out of a car and noticed the door to the place wide open."

"Male employees?" Sandra Capers was at my left side, taking down notes.

"That's correct. We're not giving out any ID's."

"What shape was Cole in when he was found?" I signaled for Ike to bring the camera and microphone.

"His exact condition, I don't have yet. I can tell you he was discovered in stall number eight, but I can't get into a lot of details."

"We know he was shot." I grabbed the microphone.

O'Donnell flipped through two pages of notes. "Before you turn those cameras on, let me recheck a few things, okay?"

"No problem," Capers said.

The crime tech stepped from the unit carrying two

brown paper bags of evidence. Ike pointed his camera in the direction of the tech and recorded her movements to the van. I noticed a face watching the collection of reporters and police through the cloud of sawdust in one of the stalls.

"I'm ready." O'Donnell lowered the legal pad. His eyes stayed forward and firm. The cameras aimed at his face. He didn't wait for a question.

"At approximately six-fifteen this morning, two men were on their way to work when they noticed a door open to the business in stall number eight. Since it's not usually open at that time, the men looked inside to find a victim, Cole Walker on the floor, bleeding. They called 911 and paramedics rushed Mr. Walker to the hospital, where he is listed in critical condition." O'Donnell paused.

"Was Walker working here? Do we know what led up to this?" Capers asked.

"From what we are told, Mr. Walker is a freelance photographer and we are checking into why he was here. The stall is rented by a company named L.M. Cornerstone Enterprises. The business here has been closed for weeks. That's why the two employees were so curious."

"Have police been here before for any reason?" Capers followed up. O'Donnell paused again, probably sorting out what he could release.

"We're checking records."

"Where's his car?" I asked.

"It hasn't been recovered. We're working on a picture for you to show what the SUV looks like and we're making an appeal to the public, if anyone has seen his car, or if anyone has any information, you're being asked to call the suspect hotline."

The questions stopped and the photographers lowered their cameras. O'Donnell took a step back.

"Can we get any closer?" I pointed to the crime tape keeping us dozens of yards from the stall door.

"Let them process it all first, then we'll see."

The image of two diamonds kept tearing at me, knowing Morgan's friendship was interfering with my job. I let it go for now.

I looked for the face behind the sawdust cloud. Ike followed me to the stall next to the crime-scene tape. I surveyed the large room. Tools were lined up on the wall in formation. Neat. Clean. Unvarnished cabinets filled one section of the room. From his sweat-stained baseball cap to the faded gym shoes, he was probably around five-foot-six. I raised my hand as a sign of greeting.

"Good morning. Busy day over here."

The dust had settled. The crease lines in his brown face converged near his chin. His hands were calloused and his eyes were the color of tea.

"Too busy for me." He adjusted a strip of sandpaper over the belt of the sander. "Too much attention."

"I'm Matt Bowens, Channel 14. We're just talking with people, trying to get an idea of what happened."

"Already talked to the police." His said the word "police" as though he had a history of bad memories with the law.

"We're not the P.D. We're just trying to figure it all out."

"There's nothing to figure out. A man got shot. Period. End of story." The sandpaper slipped off the belt. "Not now!" he shouted.

"Why don't you tighten the clamps just a bit," I offered.

"Twenty-three years of woodwork'n and you're gonna tell me how to load my sander?"

"I'm just trying—"

"What you're try'n to do is put me on that thing." He raised a dust-laden finger toward Ike's camera.

"We're just trying to find out what happened, that's all."

He put the sander down, as if he was considering my request. "I've seen you on TV before. I don't know much."

"That's okay. I just wanted to ask you what you saw when you got here, if that's okay."

Silence.

Finally, he let out a small cough. "Just a couple of questions."

Ike aimed the camera up toward his face. I eased the microphone forward. "It's usually pretty quiet here?"

"Everyone here knows everyone else. It's a small group. We all work hard. But yes, it's quiet. This is . . . this is not what we're used to."

"You see or hear anything?"

"Just what Norm and Stan said to me briefly, that they saw a man on the floor, bleeding real bad. They called police. We still can't figure out what he was doing here. The victim, I mean." The folds in his jaw stretched and punctuated each word as he spoke.

"Prior to this, let's say days and weeks ago, has there been any activity in that stall?"

"Some."

"Like what?"

"I work late and two different times, I saw bright lights coming from that stall when I went home for the night."

"Bright lights?"

His face took on the look of someone facing indecision. He said, "I think there were lights. They had a different glow than my work lights. I didn't go inside or anything."

"You see any people?"

"No. Just an SUV parked outside."

"SUV?"

"Look, I don't want to say anymore. Please, that's it."

"That's fine."

I motioned to Ike. He lowered the lens and stepped back, focusing on a wide shot.

"You mention the car to the police?"

He paused. "No. I forgot. I probably need to tell them."

"Did you get a look at anyone going in or out?"

The man waited until Ike turned off his camera before he spoke. "I didn't want to say this on camera but one night I saw a tall guy carrying out these shiny cases. I figured a new business was moving in. I didn't think anything about it."

"Thanks."

I took down his name and met Ike by the van. Sandra Capers must have started at the other end and was working her way down the stalls. A deadline was approaching.

"Let's go," I said. "We've got to feed the noon."

Chapter 6

Live truck operator Hank Fullman looked up at the forty-five-foot tall metal mast and smiled. "The signal is strong. You ready to send some video?"

I checked my watch. Ten-fifteen. "Not yet. I've got a few more minutes before we edit."

I sat at the console, thinking about the elements of the story in order to write a quick script.

"Here. This is for you." Fullman handed me a video-tape. On the cover, someone had written WALKER-HOSPITAL VIDEO. I eased the tape into the deck and pressed the play button. On the monitor, I saw two para-medics walking the gurney into the open doors of the emergency room. The video was perhaps thirty seconds. On the gurney was Cole Walker. He looked calm for someone just shot. His eyes were open and appeared alert. His right shoulder was covered in bandages. I had the sense he would recover.

Outside the truck, Fullman was in the rear making all kinds of noise, pulling out racks of cable reels. I heard a hard knock on the side of the van.

"You got your wish." O'Donnell leaned into the cavity of the live truck. "We're taking the tape down. You can move closer."

"Thanks." I said.

Two uniforms were rolling up the last of the crime tape. Ike waited with his camera. We heard a jerk and the door of metal slats lifted upward, pushed by a detective. The door produced a low screech probably from rusty ball bearings. The entire piece locked into place. Faces peaked out from the work stations.

Beyond a row of empty metal shelves, I could see blood on the concrete floor. Cole's blood. The work in the other stalls stopped and a quiet settled in, except for photographers snapping their cameras into the heads of tripods.

Cole almost died here.

The room had no furniture. A few rags were wrapped around the base of a pole. I understood why the crime techs were done so quickly. There wasn't a lot to process. They probably took a load of photographs, black powder fingerprints, DNA swabs, collected fiber, and measured off everything down to the inch. A uniform moved his car up close to the front to make sure the crime scene stayed secure and ward off any onlookers. A tech saw the open stall and grabbed her digital camera, moving from side to side, getting up to nine photographs before packing the camera away again.

"You have two minutes." The voice in my earpiece was a producer in Miami giving me countdown cues. A television monitor tuned to Channel 14 rested on the ground. I watched a string of commercials and waited for another cue. Sandra Capers was several yards from me. Both of us stood in front of a camera ready to tell South Florida all we could about the shooting of Cole Walker.

"One minute." The voice said.

I nodded to the camera.

Ike focused the camera and aimed the lens at my face. The monitor flashed images of Miami, all part of the montage of video used in the opening of the newscast. Quick flashes of letters until they all came together to form the words, Channel 14 News. I watched and heard the noon anchor, Christine Booker speak the lead-in:

"This midday, we begin our newscast with concern for one of our own. Cole Walker, a former Channel 14 photographer has been shot and is hospitalized in critical condition. Channel 14 reporter Matt Bowens is standing by in Fort Lauderdale where investigators are trying to piece together what happened . . . Matt."

"Christine, this ordeal began early this morning as police were called to this warehouse off Broward Boulevard. As you mentioned, Cole Walker, long time veteran photographer for Channel 14, who now works as a freelancer, was found here by two area employees."

As I talked, Ike panned the camera over to the empty stall.

"Police at this time do not have a motive or any suspects, but Walker was found here around six-fifteen. His car is still missing."

The director in Miami rolled the videotape of the piece Ike edited. The piece was self-contained with my voice narration and interview clips. I started with the video of Cole, then the interview with Morgan, followed with my audio track describing the police investigation. I included the interview with the cabinetmaker, and a short interview with O'Donnell. The videotape ran one minute-forty seconds. When I saw myself on TV, I started my live tag:

"And police stress that if you have any information, to please call the Suspect Hotline. Matt Bowens, Channel 14 news."

I stopped talking and I heard a soft "you're clear," in my earpiece.

I pulled out my cell phone and dialed the number to Ramon Ramirez, the Channel 14 news director. I told him everything I had so far, including Morgan's diamonds. It was my opinion to mention the gems. Leave nothing out. However, I wanted direction on whether to report the diamonds. He promised to get back to me.

I dialed Mike Brendon. The phone rang six times before he picked up.

"Matt?"

"What's up?"

"Well, for one, the police have that photograph of the SUV ready. But more important, Morgan called. Cole is awake."

Chapter 7

Fort Lauderdale Metro General Hospital was ready for us when we returned. Three security guards waved reporters to an upstairs conference room. The marketing department told us Morgan, along with Cole's doctor, would be available at a news conference.

The photogs set up a collection of microphones on a table in front of a banner touting the hospital's name in huge maroon letters. We waited twenty minutes before Morgan and the doctor walked into the room and settled in the chairs.

"My name is Doctor Reginald Flatley. To my right is Morgan Walker."

Dr. Flatley wore a starched white lab coat. His name was embroidered over his left pocket. We had interviewed him before, addressing a number of emergencies and health warnings.

"Let me start off by saying we are pleased with the progress of Mr. Walker. I want to make it clear; Mrs. Walker gave her permission for us to talk about Cole's condition. He suffered a gun shot to the right shoulder. A through-and-through wound. He is awake and his prognosis is good, in fact very good, considering. Although right now he is still in critical condition."

Dr. Flatley turned to Morgan. She moved her chair closer to the grouping of microphones. "I was very happy to see Cole open his eyes. He's under a lot of medication and they don't want him doing too much. I am thankful for the care he is getting at the hospital, and I know he will be able to come home soon. Or I should say, at some time."

Dr. Flatley leaned in toward the microphones. "A release date is a bit premature right now. What we're dealing with is keeping him stable. But we expect a full recovery."

"Are police any closer now to a motive?" Sandra Capers directed her question to Morgan.

"No. I should say, I don't know. I really haven't been in touch with them since we spoke very briefly this morning." Under the table, I saw Morgan moving her right foot in a nervous tap.

"Is Cole able to help detectives?" I asked.

Before Morgan could answer, Dr. Flatley spoke. "The police have asked us not go into what Mr. Walker is doing in regards to the investigation. All we're doing right now is making sure he is comfortable, and I'm trying to answer some of your questions regarding his immediate health."

Morgan's eyes locked on the group of reporters. "I can tell you that I know the police are doing everything they can to find who did this. I mean, I don't understand it myself. In his job, Cole has been to this very hospital many times to shoot video of people being rushed to emergency. And now we are all here talking about Cole."

Her voice softened.

Dr. Flatley interlaced his fingers. "The next few days, of course, will be critical, but I know Cole's prognosis looks good. I want to thank you for coming. If you have any other questions, please call the marketing department." He was coming up out of his seat as he said the last few words. Sandra Capers flashed me a roll of her eyes. "Not too cooperative, are they?"

"Maybe they can't be."

The lower lip of Capers stayed in a rigid line. I gave up years ago of trying to read into her face what she was planning next. I edged toward the door with the hope of getting a question to Morgan. The creased white sleeve of Dr. Flatley's coat worked like a shield for Morgan. He ushered her past me. She didn't even look in my direction. The door closed, and we were left with the rattling of photogs packing up gear.

"We get what we get." Capers snapped her pad closed.

"Maybe." I said.

Chapter 8

I placed the two candy dispensers on my desk calendar next to a coffee mug stain. One dispenser was a horse and when you pulled his head back, a mint popped out of his mouth. The other was a small plastic car.

"Do some shopping while you were out?" Mike Brendon stood over me. His glasses slid down his nose.

"Got them at the hospital gift shop. Presents."

"Where's Ike?" I asked.

"I sent him over to P.D. to get some video of the SUV they're trying to find. I thought I'd make some phone calls. Anything from Morgan?"

"No."

"Where did Channel 8 run their story?"

Brendon glanced up at the bank of televisions mounted on the wall above us. "Top story, believe it not. Even though Cole didn't work for them, they are running it pretty high."

I smelled what was left of an onion-enriched sandwich coming from Brendon's desk. My stomach gurgled a reminder that I missed lunch.

"Who is replacing you when you go to the doctor's office?" I asked.

"I'm not going. Canceled the appointment."

"Why? Sounds like it's important."

"Maybe. I reset it for later this week." Mike pulled on his beard until the strands formed a long V. "Besides, with all this stuff about Cole, I can't leave right now."

"We're fine. You can't miss appointments like that." I wanted to sound like a reasoning friend, instead of talking down to him.

"Don't worry, I'll get there."

I said, "Did they say where they want us in the ninety minutes?"

"You're in two shows. They got you as the lead at five, and you're the second story in the six. Nothing in the five-thirty."

Brendon moved back behind the wall of police scanners and telephones. "By the way, they're putting a second reporter on this. The noon anchor is doing a piece on Cole. The last couple of stories he worked on, that kind of thing."

"Does she need anything from me?"

"Not really. It's all file video with a sound byte from Ramon."

I started dialing. The voice picked up after two rings.

"Homicide."

"I'm looking for Detective Victor."

"Just a moment. Who can I say is calling?"

"Tell him it's Matt Bowens."

"Just a minute."

"Matt?"

Detective Victor had a habit of thinking about his words before he spoke.

"Afternoon. I hear Cole Walker is awake. Is he giving you a direction on suspects?"

There was a long pause. "You know I can't get into what he's saying."

"What about descriptions? If you have them, I know that's something you'd want to get out to the public."

"Well . . . we're still working on that. Because of his condition, we can't rush things."

"Do we know why he was in the warehouse?"

Another pause.

"Again, there's not too much I can share with you on that. His wife expected a call from him at about nine P.M. and we think he was in that warehouse since about three in the morning, so there's a big block of time that's unaccounted for."

I wondered if Morgan mentioned the diamonds to Victor. Just how much was she telling police?

"What about the owners of the warehouse?" I flipped my notepad back a few pages. "Anything there?"

The silence on the phone was so deep I heard paper shuffling in the background—the coming and going of detectives in the office.

"We're still tracking them down. Listen, Matt, I've got to go."

"Fine. But if you get anything on the descriptions, we can push it on the air tonight."

"We appreciate that but I'll get back to you. I promise."

"Just a couple of final things. Was there a shell casing found at the scene?"

"Okay, I'll give you one. No shell casing. But I have a question for you. Did Cole mention any problems with any clients?"

It was my turn to take some time answering.

"I asked Morgan about that. The problem is I haven't talked to Cole in a long time. And he never mentioned any hassles from clients."

"Thanks."

I asked, "Have you checked Walker's house?"

"We're using a warrant, but no, not yet."

"Thanks."

I put the phone into the cradle.

Past experience told me if Victor was close to an arrest, he wouldn't say anything. Not a word.

Morgan had a few hours, if that, before a detective would be poring over every drawer and hiding place. She had just enough time to put the videocase back or bring it to their attention.

The phone rang. Mike picked up, listened for a moment, and yelled to me. "It's Ramon."

Ramon Ramirez was in his fourth year as news director. I picked up my line. Ramon started before I stated my case. "I spoke to Morgan," Ramon began. "She called me. We have no proof the diamonds have anything to do with this shooting. We don't need to mention them now."

"With all due respect, I disagree. Yes, Cole was found miles away from his house. And I know Morgan found the diamonds at home but something is not right—"

"There is no connection," Ramon cut me off. "Matt, this sounds like a carjacking. That's it. I don't want to go on the air telling the public about his private stash until I know there is a direct connection. Until then, we honor her request and leave the information out. Are the police making a connection?"

"They don't know about the diamonds yet. She could be hiding—"

"I said the info is out." Ramon's tone was direct and final.

"And she assured me she will tell police about the gems," I responded. The conversation was over. I put the phone down.

"What's the verdict? You lose?" Mike Brendon checked his watch, then burned a look in my direction.

"No mention of the diamonds. For now."

"Too bad. Those things were big as alley roaches." Mike spread out some sheets of papers. "You ready to take some notes?" Mike Brendon summoned me over to his desk.

I flipped my pad to a clean sheet of paper.

The tips of Brendon's beard took on the hue of hot embers.

"Don't forget about Capers." Brendon's face pooled red as his beard and he shook a finger at my chest. "I don't want to see her getting something on the air before us, especially those diamonds."

"Just give me some time," I said.

We both knew sitting on information was taking a big risk. I did it all the time for major investigations where tidbits of details were kept in secret for days or months until an arrest was made. I once sat on a tip for almost two years until it was time to go public. This was different.

Mike again focused his attention on the legal pad.

"I've got a name and a home address. This is the listed taxpayer of that warehouse unit where Cole was found. As soon as Ike comes back, you can check it out."

Chapter 9

The townhouse was so close to the ocean, I smelled the salty mist of the Atlantic. Crescent View Manor was in full view when Ike eased the van past a row of seagrape trees and parked. The lot surface was covered with wet spots from a quick hit of rain and dozens of dead brown leaves stuck to the moistened pavement.

"Two ten," I told Ike. "It's the one on the corner."

Each townhouse was identical except for the address. Ike positioned the camera on his shoulder and kept the lens down. As I walked to the door, a woman emerged from her townhouse, carrying a large watering jug. She adjusted the wide brim sunhat on her head until I could see the gray glint in her eyes, watching me from her front sidewalk.

I reached the door of Roland Campton and knocked. I waited thirty seconds or so, then rang the doorbell. No answer. I knocked again and rang the doorbell one more time. There were no sounds coming from the house. No dogs barking. I glanced at the windows, looking for a finger parting the blinds. Nothing. The parking space near the front door was empty. I stepped back from the door and walked toward the woman in the hat.

"Ever see your neighbor?" I asked.

"Mr. Campton? Not for awhile."

"Awhile?"

"Yes, well I haven't seen him for days now."

I checked the window. Still no movement.

"Do you know anything about him or what he does for a living?" I kept glancing from her to the window and the door. She lowered her water jug to the ground. I guessed she was in her sixties. She wore gardening gloves and kept pulling at the length of her sleeves until the exposed skin was covered. The woman followed my stare to her hands.

"Doctor says I shouldn't be in the sun. But tending to my roses is what I like to do. What was your question again?"

"Your neighbor, Roland Campton, do you know what he does for a living?"

"Not really. We don't talk that much. Is there a problem?"

"No problem just yet. I'm Matt Bowens with Channel 14, and I'd like to talk to Mr. Campton. Let me give you my card." I reached into my wallet for a business card. "If he shows up, could you please give me a call?"

"Sure. I guess so."

The afternoon was unproductive. I called the hospital several times but Morgan never returned my messages. Besides the neighbor, I left a business card on Roland Campton's door, but he didn't call. Patrick O'Donnell had nothing new to add to his earlier interview, and Detective Victor was out of the office the three times I checked. My stories at 5 and 6 PM became repeats of what I had in the noon newscast.

There would be a day two of the story, and tomorrow morning I'd start fresh.

Chapter 10

I smelled her fragrance before she leaned in to kiss me. Cat Miller stood back, inspecting me as if a shirt out of place or a sagging brow could tell her how my day had progressed. The pulse and beat of Usher rumbled from the speakers.

"I heard about your photographer. Terrible. Any leads?"

"Nothing yet." My mind was still focused on the image of Cat's lips pulling away from me, and I stepped forward to make another connection but she was gone, headed in the direction of the aroma coming from the kitchen. She took four steps, then stopped. Her head turned toward the sounds of a video game coming from the bedroom.

"What did I tell you?"

"Mom." The moan was slow and drawn out.

"You know what I told you. Homework first, video games come later. Now turn it off."

"Mom, can I finish—"

"Now!" There was snap and finality in her voice. I eased close enough to the room to see a car on the television screen positioned on a race track. The low roar of an engine filled the room. Suddenly the screen went black.

"What's up, Jason?"

"Hi Matt." The six-year old flashed a quick smile before digging into his book bag.

"That boy, I just don't know." Cat was talking to herself, and shaking her head.

"Shauna?" Cat shouted so loud, my eyes widened.

"Yeah." The voice came from another room in the house.

"Don't forget, we have the dentist tomorrow."

"I know." The voice was faint.

Cat Miller was a divorced parent of two. I admired her for graduating from college and pursuing a career with two kids in elementary school. She constantly teased me, predicting I'd find someone else and leave her. Once she told me she didn't come with strings attached, hers were ropes.

Cat pushed a large wooden spoon into a pot and stirred hard until small waves of mashed potatoes washed up against the sides. On the stove the smells overwhelmed the kitchen.

"You ready?" Cat's smile arched back into the brown sheen of her cheeks. I was locked on her eyes. They were hazel and the reason for her nickname. No one called her Yvonne. Only Cat.

"I'm ready. I think."

"Think?" Her smile was gone. "The kids have been looking forward to this for months. That's all they've been talking about."

"Don't worry, it's set. I have the eighth off. But you know about the news business."

"Believe me, I know." Cat increased the speed of her circular whips. The spoon knocked against the sides of the pot with authority, the sounds bouncing off the wall. "I remember waiting for you for two hours at the restaurant. I'm sitting at the bar, then of all things, I look up and see you on television." Her last few words spiked up to a higher octave.

"I couldn't get out of it. A plane landed on the turnpike. I had to go."

She looked at me through the steam rising from the mashed potatoes.

"And three weeks ago, you promised to speak to Shauna's class. You were a no-show."

"I apologized, Cat. I'll say it again, I'm sorry. If there's something going on out there and I have to cover it, I've got to go."

The edges around her eyes softened. She placed the spoon on a small plate next to the front burner and wriggled off the cooking mitt from her left hand. She sighed. "I guess you're right. I know you're right. Your job comes first. But after dealing for so long with their sorry excuse of a father . . ."

I stepped in close, turning her toward me, and catching her before she could say another word, letting the kiss linger long enough to feel her hands trace the curve of my back. I just wanted to hold her. Finally, I eased back and whispered into her cheek.

"I know I wasn't there all those times. It's just—"

"Your job?" She said. Cat moved a bit away from me. "I don't understand the hours, but I'm trying."

In a year of dating, I stood her up twelve times. Maybe more. Each missed rendezvous became a red flag in the relationship, dragging us into a schism we both knew could force one of us into a decision about our future.

I met Cat in a singles bar, and two weeks later, I packed away my dating book and put the collection of names and numbers in a shoebox stacked next to some old shirts that didn't fit anymore and a folder filled with tax returns.

Her hazel eyes flickered between me and the pork chops simmering in the skillet. Her skin reflected dark brown in the kitchen light. I pushed away, giving her more space to stack plates. She smiled at me and worked in silence, finally wiping her hands down with a towel.

"Jason, Shauna." Cat stood in the hallway and shouted to the bedrooms. Ten-year old Shauna ambled to the table, flipping an errant black pigtail behind her back. No sign of Jason. The smell of the chops turned the juices loose in my stomach. Cat lowered each plate into position on the table and the food gave the room a certain warmth.

"Jason, we're all waiting." Cat's voice was low and even, as though he was getting the last warning before consequences were meted out.

She placed a bowl of water in the center of the table. An array of gardenia blossoms floated on the surface. "I need your advice," she said, admiring the white petals. "G.G. is coming over later; there's a very important decision I have to make."

G.G. always left me with a sense of someone in control. In terms of simple determination, G.G. Everson was the strongest person I had ever met. Cat and G.G. grew up in Fort Lauderdale. Cat patted a stack of papers. "After dinner, I want you to read this." There was excitement in Cat's voice. The top page looked like a drawing of a yard.

"You two have a project in mind?"

"It's a bit stronger than that. You see this?" Cat pulled out a page from the stack. "This is what we have in mind."

"We?"

"I worked this out with G.G. You see this right here?" She pointed to the center of the page. Before I could answer her, my cell phone hummed against my side.

"Excuse me for a second." I reached for my phone and recognized the number to the newsroom.

"Matt?"

"Yes?"

"Sorry to bother you. I never made it out of the office. I hate to do this but I'd like to send you somewhere," Brendon said.

"Can't the night crew pick this up? What's going on?"

"They found Cole's car."

"Where?"

I realized I practically shouted the word, and Cat's sparkling eyes blinked hard.

"It's in the parking garage of the Clarkston Hotel, you know, down by A1A, close to the water. I really hate to do this to you, but can Ike meet you at the scene?"

"No problem. I'll be there."

"One other thing," Brendon paused.

Cat's expression said put away the phone. Now.

"Look, Mike, I need a minute. Let me call you in the car in a few minutes. I'll be there." I ended the call and eased the cell phone into my pocket.

"But Matt." Cat's face had a look of dejection. The room seemed just a bit hotter. I could only see half her eyes. Her eyelids were covering part of the usual glow.

"I have to go," I said.

Silence.

I said, "It's about the Walker case. They're sending me to a scene. I'm sorry. This is really important."

"Call me later. I'll be up." Her words were soft. She never got up from her chair, staying fixed in front of the plates. She stroked ebony fingers against her cheeks and stared at the floor. "We really have to talk," she said.

"Bye Matt." Shauna had the same hazel eyes as her mother.

I pulled out the candy I bought at the hospital and placed the plastic dispensers on the table. Shauna's eyes glowed and she let out a small gasp. She reached for the candy.

"After dinner," Cat scolded. "What do you say?" Cat looked at Shauna.

"Thank you," she said.

I almost bumped into Jason in the hallway. He was in a full run but he managed to stop. "You ready for the trip?" he said, looking up at me. I hesitated before answering his question.

"I'll be there."

When I reached the door, I heard voices saying grace. I turned the knob and stepped into the radiance of a street light.

I tapped out the numbers to the newsroom on my phone. After three rings, Mike answered. I dug for my car keys.

"Okay, what's the deal?"

Mike gathered a chest full of air before he spoke.

"They found Cole's car. And inside they found a body."

Chapter 11

The south side of the Clarkston Hotel opened to the brackish water of the New River of Fort Lauderdale. Shards of gray clouds lined up against the night sky. I got out of the car to street smells of suntan lotion, saltwater, and brine-soaked sand.

"Over here." Ike Cashing directed me past three unmarked police cars.

"Whatcha got?" I asked.

"Take a look through here." Ike stepped away from the camera mounted on a tripod. I looked into the one-inch viewing monitor and saw a blue SUV parked next to a pole in the parking lot. A collection of bright forensic lights stood to the right side, basking the parking lot and the SUV in white. A crime scene technician aimed a digital camera, taking a photograph of something on the ground. The victim was slumped over in the passenger side of the car. The crime tech took another picture, flooding the area with light for just a millisecond.

The tech tugged on his gloves and opened the car door

wide to reveal a crimson spiderweb of blood dripping down a tan interior.

I leaned back from the camera.

"Did anyone say how long the car has been there?" I turned my gaze in the direction of the parking lot. "What I mean is, has it been there for as long as Cole has been in the hospital?"

"The PIO hasn't been out here to tell us anything." Ike leaned into his camera, putting his arm around the housing and repositioning the angle. I looked around for any witnesses.

A small crowd had gathered near the crime tape. Ike said, "Stuff's happening. They got a bunch of uniforms out searching every bit of the garage. There's a few people who don't mind being interviewed and the PIO will be here in ten minutes."

I glanced at my watch. Eight-fifteen. I decided to give myself twenty minutes before I called the night producer. "Where are the interviews?"

"You've got two right there and another over near the first police car."

Ike unsnapped his camera from the tripod.

"Lead the way," I said.

I interviewed a couple from New York and a paint salesman who was spending time walking the beach. They all expressed a certain shock acknowledging the taking of a life in the midst of palm trees and wind swept beaches. I looked at the Clarkston Hotel and wondered how the body of a man in an SUV fit into the whole picture. How was Cole involved?

"I didn't think I'd see you again so soon." Patrick O'-

Donnell pulled a pen from his pocket and started to scribble something on a single sheet of yellow paper.

"What have you got?" I flipped open my pad to a clean page.

"Well, hopefully I can tell you a bit more than I could this afternoon. First of all, we're holding the name on the victim but we do have some information about him." O'-Donnell folded the paper and stuffed it in his pocket. "I'm ready."

Ike aimed the camera at O'Donnell.

"A hotel guest noticed something strange about the SUV parked in the lot here at the Clarkston Hotel. He notified the hotel and they went out to investigate. They found a man in the passenger seat who had blood on his shirt. When they couldn't get the door open, they called 9-1-1. Upon opening the door, paramedics determined the victim had expired and detectives and crime-scene units were brought in. The man is considered a homicide victim but we can't give out too many details yet on his cause of death."

"Is this Cole Walker's SUV?" I asked.

"The only thing I can tell you is that we are no longer putting out the message that we're looking for that car."

"Is that Cole's car?"

"Until we get a final determination from homicide, I can't confirm that, but again, we pulled our state wide bulletin for the missing car."

"Is Cole Walker considered a suspect at this time?"

"The only thing I can tell you for certain is that we plan to speak to Mr. Walker."

"And what about the victim? What can you tell us?"

"Well, I can tell you that he is local. We have not found

his car, but in the morning we can provide you more details on that. When he was last seen, he was carrying a briefcase, and we are putting out the word to the public to call us if they have any information about the case."

"A briefcase?"

"Yes. Besides homicide this is also being worked as a robbery. The value of the items inside the case is being listed at more than three-hundred-fifty thousand dollars. The victim was a diamond courier and a bag of cut gems is missing."

Chapter 12

I took a small step back and glanced at Ike. He showed no emotion from behind the camera. My pause gave Patrick a reason to stop the interview.

"You done?"

"Just a few more questions. Was the victim staying at the hotel?"

"Yes. We know he checked in sometime this afternoon and we are talking to witnesses to see when, and if, he had any guests."

"Does the hotel have camera surveillance?"

"I'll check, but in the parking lot, I don't think so." He paused. "Maybe in the lobby, but that's part of the investigation."

"Suspects?"

"At this time, no. Not even a description. That's why we need some help on this. We know it's not unusual for a diamond courier or salesman to meet with someone in a hotel room and conduct business. But how Mr. Cole's SUV plays a part in all this is still a matter to be investigated."

"Is Cole's shooting connected to the diamond theft and this murder?"

"We can't answer that yet."

"About the diamonds, what—"

He cut me off. "Nothing more on the diamonds. Check with me tomorrow."

"Did you know Morgan Walker found some rather large diamonds herself?"

O'Donnell's face showed no emotion. "I have no information on that."

"Have you checked with her about the diamonds she has?"

"Like I said," O'Donnell started, "I don't know anything about that. But I promise to get back to you." He turned away from me. Ike powered down his camera. I lowered my microphone but I tossed more questions at Patrick. "Have you talked with Morgan?"

"Mrs. Walker? No. Her time should be at the hospital. We understand that, and we know we can approach her tomorrow sometime."

"So, she hasn't given detectives a lot of information?"

"I can answer that by saying no, she hasn't. But at the same time, I have no way of knowing what she is saying to homicide and if I did, I couldn't pass it on anyway."

"What about the house? Have you checked it yet?"

"We serve the warrant in the morning. I think someone is contacting Mrs. Walker to make sure she is there." O'-Donnell left but he assured me he would stay in the area for another thirty minutes or so.

I called Mike Brendon, who was still working the assignment desk. My conversation was short. I stuffed the cell phone in my pocket.

Ike leveled the first question at me.

"So, we can talk about the diamonds?" Ike asked.

"Yes." I said. It was too easy to second-guess the news director on Morgan's diamonds. I never wanted to hold out the information but now I was worn down. I was hungry, and doubt was creeping into my mind.

"Mike says Ramon gave us the clearance to go with the information, but he stands by his earlier decision to hold off on the info."

"Have you heard from Morgan?" Ike's words came at me while he moved the camera back in position to see the work of the crime-scene techs.

"She's my next phone call."

Crews from two other news stations and the newspapers were gathering a few yards from us. O'Donnell was doing interviews with them, probably going through the same series of questions and answers.

I dialed the number to the hospital nurse's desk for ICU. After a long wait, the nurse on duty agreed to ask for Morgan. A few more minutes passed. Morgan answered.

"Do you know what's happened out here?" I started.

"If you mean Cole's car, yes, I already heard. If police won't confirm it, I will. It's Cole's SUV."

"How is Cole?"

"Better. He said a few words then drifted off into a deep sleep. He's not in a coma or anything, it's just that his body needs the rest."

"He say anything to police?"

"Not yet. They're being very patient."

"Morgan, we need to talk."

"I know what you're going to say, Matt. I called the police and told them about the diamonds. Thank you for waiting. I just wasn't sure. It's just that—" She paused. "There is still no connection between the diamonds I have, Cole, or the crime scene at the hotel."

I heard Morgan breathing into the phone. Labored, anxious breaths of someone who was falling to another rung.

"You okay, Morgan?"

"Not really. The police say I can give them the diamonds in the morning when they do their search. But you said I could ask for a favor."

"What is it?"

"Just see me to my door. I don't want to drive."

"I don't get off until after eleven."

"It doesn't matter, I'll wait."

"You can always call police—"

"No. If you can Matt, I want you there."

"No problem."

At exactly 11:01 P.M., I told a south Florida television audience everything I knew about the Cole Walker case. The SUV, the body inside, and the shooting of Cole. I talked about the diamond find by Morgan and the theft of diamonds from the courier's briefcase. I made it clear I couldn't make any connection between the two until I got that from police.

Not long after I was finished with my report, I felt my cell phone vibrate. I answered.

"Matt, I know it's late but I thought we might get together." Cat's voice sounded alluring. "The kids are in bed, and I'm up doing some work."

"I'm sorry about dinner," I said.

"I understand. So, are you coming over? We never had our talk. I really need your input." Images of Cat peppered my thoughts until I remembered the phone call from the hospital.

"I promised Morgan Walker I would see her home, then I'm free."

"Who?"

I explained the day that started with diamonds rolling on a carpet.

"We're not having much luck, are we?" Cat's voice was barely audible.

"I promise I'll be there after I get off tomorrow."

"Fine. Good night, Matt."

Ike told me to leave and get some food. He remained in place to record video of the body being removed by the medical examiner, and the the crime techs towing Cole's SUV to be checked for fingerprints and evidence.

Chapter 13

Morgan was waiting for me in front of the emergency room entrance. Through the double glass doors, I saw a uniform walking the hallway. A single ambulance was parked off to the right. A paramedic was spraying down his gurney with disinfectant. The place was quiet.

"Thanks," Morgan closed the door, leaned back in the seat, and closed her eyes. "I am so tired."

She pulled the seat belt in place then dragged her hands down her face. "Maybe you can make some sense out of all this, because I can't." Morgan looked directly at me. Her eyes now open, looking worn. The makeup was gone and her blouse had a smudge just above the waist.

"The main thing is that Cole is getting the medical attention he needs," I said.

"That's just it." Morgan's voice rose. "It could have been worse."

"Any idea what Cole was doing at the warehouse?"

Morgan didn't answer right away. "I'm still trying to figure that out. While he was sleeping, I kept going over it.

Why would his car end up in that parking lot? With a body inside? There has to be a connection with the diamonds."

"When the name of the victim is released, we can check it against any records Cole has at home."

"He's the worst when it comes to things like that. Most of it, he just keeps in his head."

The next few miles, I let the music on the radio fill the silence. Morgan folded her arms and stared into the night. I kept thinking about the interview with the cabinetmaker at the warehouse. He referred to shiny cases coming out of the warehouse. Those could have been cases for studio lights. Ike had a set in his SUV. The light stand extends and lights attach at the top. It would explain the bright lights he saw one night. I reasoned Cole was probably hired by someone to shoot a video sequence at the warehouse. He might have needed the light kit to brighten up the subject. But what was he shooting? What did Cole get himself into?

Morgan turned toward me. "I need another favor."

"Every time you say that, I sense a problem."

"I need someone with me. We need to make a short stop before you take me home."

I felt myself sliding down a slope of trouble. "Where?" I said.

"I need to meet someone at the Diamond-Escape, Ltd. Is that okay?"

"Let's think about this for a moment." I slowed the car down. "What will they tell us?"

"Please, just let me follow through on this." The street lights and shadows moved across her face.

"It's close to midnight," I said.

"Someone is waiting for us."

* * *

The Diamond-Escape, Ltd was the last store in a line of shops in a one block area just north of downtown Fort Lauderdale. A single light came from somewhere in the back of the store. A two-foot tall neon sign, DIAMOND-ESCAPE, was dark. I parked the car next to a black Lexus. Morgan opened the car door and was out before I got the beemer stopped.

A few seconds after she knocked on the glass door, I heard movement from inside. Heavy bolt locks turned. The door opened to a voice and a hand gesturing us to come inside.

"It's okay. Just let me lock up behind you." The voice was heavy, a bit strained probably from years of smoking. I guessed he was five-six. His brown eyes were trapped behind thick glasses and a tuft of white hair pushed up from the top of his beach shirt.

"Thank you for doing this." Morgan left the both of us and took up a chair near an empty display case.

"Naw, not here," he said. "Let's go to the back. I don't want anyone to think we're open." We followed him down a narrow hallway to an office. He gestured again. This time to a pair of plastic lawn chairs, each with a faded blue seat cushion.

"Matt, I'd like you to meet Sankerman Dobb."

"Evening." He folded his arms for just seconds before letting them settle behind his back. He turned to Morgan. "I haven't seen you since you and Cole picked out a ring."

I reached to shake his hand. "I already know who you are, Mr. Bowens. Channel 14, I believe."

"That's correct."

His hands were free of any jewelry. Not even a wedding band. He was smiling, even though there was nothing to ignite a laugh.

"So, Mrs. Walker, what do you have to show me? I couldn't tell very much by your phone call."

Morgan reached into her purse and withdrew the envelope I gave her. She placed it on the desk, then pushed the envelope flat on a green square of felt and kept her palm pressed hard against the paper. "I just want an honest assessment of what I've got. And we're done."

"No problem." The deep gravel of a voice sounded defensive. "All I believe in is honesty. That's how I built up my shop."

Morgan lifted her hand, leaving the envelope. Dobb stared at the top of the desk. He carefully lifted the envelope and let the contents roll out onto the felt.

"My, my," he said. "This was worth staying up for."

Under the soft lights, the diamonds lit up. They looked brighter now than in the newsroom lighting.

"And where did you say you got these?" Dobb's stare was intense.

"I don't want to get into that right now." Morgan's face had an odd expression, like someone who wanted to rethink the last five minutes.

"May I?" Dobb pointed to the diamonds, as if to pick them up.

"Go right ahead," Morgan said. "That's why we're here."

"Just let me get my loupe in place." He raised the viewing glass to his eye and picked up one jewel, moving his hand closer until the gem was an inch or so from his face.

"Round cut," he whispered. "Very good job. There must be seventy facets here. That's a lot. The standard is around fifty-two." Dobb twisted the diamond, savoring the angles. He made the diamond dip and sparkle. His smile reached high up into the corners of his jaw.

He put the diamond down.

"Well, what do you think? What did you see?" Morgan shifted in the chair.

"Well, first, it's what I don't see. I've never seen a diamond like this. This is the finest."

Dobb picked up the diamond again and pushed it close to his eye and the loupe. "I don't see any inclusions. No flaws, not one. And the color is, how can I say this, perfect. Maybe beyond perfect."

Morgan reached for the second diamond.

"Can I check that one as well?" Dobb moved his eye from the loupe and concentrated on Morgan.

"You've been very helpful," Morgan said. She slid her hand over the diamond.

"Now, I came back and opened up for you. It's very late. At least you can let me take a look." Dobb's smile was gone. The edges of his lips drew inward, his eyes locked on Morgan. She pulled her hand back to reveal the second stone.

"Okay, a quick look."

Dobb picked up the second gem. He rotated the diamond slowly. "This is just fantastic."

Morgan snatched the diamond from him. "That's enough," she shouted.

"But I haven't—"

"We're done here." Morgan swept the remaining diamond from the table, dropping both of them in the envelope and rising from her chair at the same time.

"But please, you must let me get a better look. I have some other equipment, my microscope. Please, if you will let me."

Morgan said, "Sorry, we've got to be going. Like you said, it's late."

Morgan was in the hallway, stepping past the darkened display cabinets, tucking the diamonds away in her purse. I kept up with her, and Dobb was a close third.

"Why won't you let me examine them? Do you know how much these diamonds are worth?" Dobb reacted like the diamonds were more important than his shop or the air he breathed. Somehow he moved past us in the narrow hallway. Bodies sliding and jostling against the wall. Morgan opened the front door. Dobb pressed a hand against the door, slamming it shut.

"Let me out." Morgan's voice echoed in the room. Dobb finally pulled his hand down.

"Will you at least think about letting me see them again?" he asked.

"I can't promise that." Morgan opened the door and was standing in front of the Beemer before I had a chance to pull out my keys. Dobb was standing there, framed in the doorway.

"Just two things," I said. I opened her door and waited until I started the motor. "First, what are you hiding? Are you still trying to protect Cole? And second, everything I saw in there is on the record. I'm not holding back anything."

Morgan's firm look she had given Dobb was now directed at me. I didn't care anymore. The courtesy of friendship was worn out. "Why come here if you didn't want him to see both diamonds?" I asked.

"I didn't need his help anymore."

"Well, would you mind helping me out? What's the deal on the diamonds?"

"I wanted to check them out before I turn them over to the police." She paused. "I don't know if I can trust you anymore, Matt."

"And who is the one who trusted you?"

"You say everything is on the record?"

"Everything."

"You can report anything you saw," she said.

"I plan to do just that."

"And I plan to wait before answering your next question."

Chapter 14

Morgan turned her head into the car seat and closed her eyes. Within minutes, her breathing was even and relaxed. I didn't want to wake her up. I traveled up the interstate for two miles before reaching the exit and turning off.

"We're here," I said. When she didn't respond the first time, I gave her shoulder a soft tap. "Morgan."

"Oh, thanks."

I reasoned I would call Cat once Morgan was inside.

Her home was typical of south Florida—concrete block smothered in stucco and painted a bright color to reflect the hot sun. I didn't want to check my watch, but it was probably close to 1 A.M. when Morgan got out of the car, walked a few steps, turned the key, and stepped into the dark hallway. I followed her.

"Don't mind the mess on the floor. I was in a hurry when I left out of here." The living room was small. On the left I saw French doors, leading to a den. One side of the wall was filled with shelves of videotapes. Hundreds of them.

"Is that where you found the diamonds?"

"Yes." Morgan stared at the general direction of the tapes. She stood there trancelike, fixated on the entrance. A faint night-light stuck in a socket provided a soft glow, just enough to see the inside of the room.

"Let me just get a light on."

From the living room I could see just about every corner of the house. She walked to the kitchen and stopped. Morgan's right arm raised in the direction of the rear of the kitchen.

"I don't remember the back door being open—"

Morgan's steps picked up in speed with each pace. She reached the door and stopped.

"You were in a hurry this morning. Maybe you left it that way?"

"I'm sure I locked that door."

I motioned to her not to move. From my spot near the entrance to the kitchen, I could see the door. Morgan stood motionless.

I listened to the house. The soft hum of an air-conditioning unit came from somewhere in the rear of the building. I looked around the kitchen and through the window over the sink. Nothing. Morgan angled her body in front of the window and stared. I moved next to her. Just feet from the window, a collection of palm trees waved palm fronds at the street light.

"You noticed anything in the wrong place? Something knocked over?" I glanced back down the hallway.

Even though Morgan said she left a mess, I didn't see it. The ceramic tile floor was clean. The counter was wiped down. No clothes left by the bedroom door.

"What's over here?" I pointed to a second door in the kitchen.

"That leads to the garage."

The hum of the air-conditioner stopped.

"Does that door have a dead bolt?"

"No."

"What about the den?"

"We always keep it open."

Morgan used her index finger to turn on a light. The room stayed dark. "Oh great. Now what?"

She flipped the switch a few times. No light.

"We just had the air on, so something is up." I stepped toward the den. The clock mounted in the stove was not running. The second hand was locked in position.

"Where's your breaker switches?" I asked.

"In the garage."

"I know the main power lever is outside, but which wall?"

"I don't know. Let me think." Morgan rubbed at her temples. "The south wall, I think."

"Someone might be outside, turning off the power."

I was right outside the den. The night-light was out. I moved past the open set of French doors. I couldn't see much. The single source of outside light, a window in the back of the room, was covered with a set of blinds. Morgan was right behind me. I pulled out my cell phone and handed it to Morgan. "I don't want to call 911 unless we have a real emergency—but just in case. You have any flashlights?"

"In the desk."

I bumped my right foot on the leg of the desk. Morgan pulled out the desk drawer. I heard the scraping of fingers jabbing at pencils and paperwork in the drawer.

"I got it."

I took the flashlight and thumbed for the on switch. A

beam of soft light lit up a corner of the room. I walked the beam slowly against the shelves of videotape boxes.

"Does everything look right?"

Morgan didn't answer. I moved the beam from the ceiling and down to the floor.

"Something . . ." Morgan started. "I moved some of these boxes myself. If I only had more light."

I stepped away from her until I reached the window. Once the blinds were pulled to the side, I checked other houses. The one next to us was dark. Two houses over, a light shone over the front entrance.

"Maybe the power just went out and that's all." The beam cast an eerie shadow on Morgan's face, distorting her eyes and cutting deep pools of jagged shadows in place of her cheeks. I checked the room with the flashlight.

"Matt!" Morgan screamed.

"What? Where?"

Morgan jerked her arm upward, pointing in the direction of the window. "Someone was there!"

"Stay here."

I gave the flashlight to Morgan and ran to the front door. I tried to remember the layout of the house to avoid running into a table. I managed to get the doorknob to twist, turn and open in a single motion.

I didn't stop until I got ready to turn the corner. I paused and peeked around the side of the building. I didn't know what to expect. There was no moonlight to help me. Hearing nothing, I edged around the corner of the house. There were just palm trees. I stepped to the window outside the den. The tall grass meant there would be no footprints, if someone was really there. I kept going until I reached the main power lever. It was in the off position. I pushed up on the lever until it locked into place. Immediately, the air-conditioner kicked back on.

Then I heard it.

The sound came from behind me. A soft rustle at first, then loud catches of something heavy moving away from me, finally fading in the distance. And gone.

Morgan.

I ran back to the front of the house and looked for the beam from the flashlight. Anything to tell me she was safe. The front door was open.

Did I leave it like that?

Morgan's shape filled up a portion of the door space. The glow of the inside house lights formed an outline of her body.

"I saw something," she whispered. "I know I did."

I again turned my attention toward the movement, stepping off a quick pace until a ficus bush blocked me. If anyone was there, he got away.

In Florida once the sun dropped, anything could be moving. The urban environment gave way to the animals.

"I know what I saw," Morgan said. Her eyes no longer held fear. She had an even tone in her voice like someone resigned to a certain fate. Morgan never blinked.

"And he had a tattoo on his arm."

Chapter 15

Morgan didn't want to stay at her home. I drove her to a hotel a mile east, helped her check in, then turned the Beemer toward the ocean. Morgan called the police and a unit checked the back of her place and found nothing.

It was just past 3 A.M. when I reached my apartment. Too late to call Cat. I passed on a glass of white Zinfandel and instead fired up my stereo, letting the tones of Luther Vandross fill the room. I played a voice message from Cat, telling me to reach her sometime during the day.

My sixth-floor apartment had a view of Fort Lauderdale Beach. I stepped out onto the balcony and sucked in a chest full of cool predawn air. The breeze always made me sleepy, and right now I needed its mercurial effect.

The dream I had that night resembled many others. I kept going over the moments before I was shot and tried to place a face with the gun aimed at my chest. Weeks before the shooting, I had a run-in with a drug dealer named Mushmouth. Was he the shooter? My mind tried to focus on the shadows behind the gun, only to fail to put together a picture of the man responsible for pulling the trigger.

I skipped breakfast, joined Ike, and we met Morgan in front of her house.

"They told me they couldn't find anything." Morgan's eyes showed a night's full of worry. She pointed to the back of the house. "I know I saw someone."

Ike set up his camera on a shot of Morgan's house. Two uniforms were walking from the rear to their marked units. They prepared to leave. I heard the light clatter of people inside.

"What time did they come to serve the warrant?" I said.

"They were here waiting for me when I got home from the hotel. I took a cab to pick up my car and they were here. That must have been around 7 A.M."

"What about the diamonds?"

"They took a hard look at them and bagged them up." Morgan squinted, then put her right hand up to her forehead, forming her fingers like an awning to block out the morning sun. "If we scared off someone, they must have been looking for something."

"How is Cole?"

"I'm due at the hospital in a couple of hours. I've got to do something first."

"Did the police say anything about the gems?" I asked.

"No. But I told them everything. I mentioned the jeweler we saw last night."

"But you cut him off. He was about to say something about the quality."

Morgan dropped her hand to her side and stepped back

into a shadow. "Whatever he was about to say, I didn't want to hear it."

"Even if it has a direct bearing on Cole's situation?"

Morgan shook her head.

"What about the other tape boxes? Any diamonds in them?"

"Nothing," Morgan said. "Just the one box."

Columns of gray clouds were bunched to one side of the sky.

"I guess I missed you last night." Sandra Capers unfolded a page of her notepad. Her eyes were as serious as a last wish.

Morgan moved away from us, headed for the front door, whispering, "No interviews." She didn't look back.

Sanders stared at me. I said, "Where were you?" I studied her eyes. They had the calm demeanor of the best bluff at the poker table.

"The situation at the hotel? They didn't call me and someone else covered it," she said. "I saw your report at eleven. A body in Cole's car? How does that happen?" The wind kicked at the loose strands of Sandra's hair.

"Maybe we'll know today."

I was used to working against Capers. Most of the south Florida TV reporters worked out of the main stations in Miami. The newsrooms maintained a small satellite station in Fort Lauderdale and that meant fewer people. I was left battling Sandra on stories almost on a daily basis. We worked the streets during the day, and Mike Brendon compared our stories in the evening newscasts.

Ike approached. "Mike wants you to give him a call."

He picked up on the second ring. I heard noises and several voices in the background. "What's going on?" I asked.

"They're installing that camera on the roof and they're not too quiet about it. Listen, the police are set to have a news conference in an hour. They want to release the latest on the body found in the car. Expect a live hit in the noon newscast from the police station."

I didn't leave Morgan's house until I was reasonably sure I wouldn't miss something. I still expected a phone call if the warrant turned up something major.

The police station was a few miles to the east, near the site of a boarded-up schoolhouse. A community-service aide directed news crews to the second floor.

Ike set up a tripod in the conference room. Faded off-white walls surrounded us. Posters of anti-drunk driving campaigns were tacked up on either side of the door. Two long folding tables served as the speakers' platform. Ike placed his microphone in the center of the tables. Sandra Capers and her photog were next into the room. They were soon followed by reporters from the newspapers and two radio stations. A collection of microphones were grouped together.

Patrick O'Donnell peeked into the room. He held up his hand. "Five minutes."

We acknowledged his warning and he disappeared behind the door. Fifteen minutes later, he emerged and stood before the microphones. A semicircle of cameras aimed at his face.

"Here's what I can give you. The victim has been identified as Grant Parkin. From what we can put together, Mr. Parkin was set to meet a customer at the Clarkston Hotel. From witnesses and other information, the meeting did take place. There was no transaction and Mr. Parkin headed out to leave. The next few minutes are still in question, but we theorize Mr. Parkin met someone else in the parking lot and they made off with his briefcase after shooting the victim."

"How did he end up in Cole Walker's car?" I asked.

"We're still going over the SUV, but there's a possibility the meeting took place in the car."

I said, "Your direct tie between the two shootings is Cole Walker's car. Are we looking at one person doing the shootings?"

"I can't answer that right now."

"And this meeting in the car . . . was this before or after Cole Walker was shot?"

O'Donnell took some time before answering my question. "We're still working ballistics and an exact time line. We also checked Mr. Walker's hands for gunshot residue, or GSR, so I don't want to speculate on that. We should know something soon."

"But there's a chance any gun shot residue was washed off?" I asked.

"Again, we are checking."

Capers asked, "Anything new on the missing diamonds?"

"There's not a lot we can give you in that area. The diamonds were loose, not mounted in a ring. Again, all cut diamonds. They ranged in size from one-half to two carats each."

Even though the diamonds Morgan showed me were much larger than the missing jewels, there was still a question. I took a small step forward. "Are the diamonds owned by Morgan Walker connected in any way to the missing gems?"

"Before we answer that, we need the briefcase of diamonds, and we need to speak to Cole Walker. Until then, I'm not going to speculate on whether there is a connection."

"Was Grant Parkin a part of L.M. Cornerstone?" The question came from Sandra Capers.

"As far we know, he was not." O'Donnell waved his right hand at the bank of cameras. "That's all I've got. I'll be passing out information about Parkin."

O'Donnell opened a folder on the table and gave each of us a one page description of what happened, along with Grant Parkin's address.

Chapter 17

An irregular-shaped pond of algae-stained water bordered a yellow stucco home, trimmed in beige paint. Ike rolled to a stop behind the news van of Sandra Capers. I got out, Ike got his camera gear, and we joined Capers at the door. Sandra touched the doorbell at the home of Grant Parkin. I was already prepared to leave and go back to the van. A few seconds passed, then I thought I heard movement from behind the front bay window.

The door opened.

Her hair was long, perhaps down to her waist. She pushed a side of her dark locks to one side, revealing cobalt blue eyes.

"I know why you're here. C'mon in." She directed us to the family room, where a wrap-around couch took up a full third of the space. The faint aroma of day old roses drifted from somewhere in the kitchen. I followed her gaze to the vase. She let her eyes rest on the grouping of flowers, then back to us.

"He just gave me those," she said.

We introduced ourselves. Sandra Capers fidgeted on the balls of her running shoes.

"My name is Amelia Parkin. The reason I want to speak to you is because I want to find out who did this. Where do you want to do the interview?"

Ike pointed to a leather chair in the corner. She sat down while the photographers set up their gear.

"Do you have a picture of your husband?" I asked her.

"Can I get up for a moment?"

"Sure."

Amelia Parkin rose from the chair and left the room as easy as a model stepping onto the runway. She had a certain poise about her, a casual demeanor that kept you thinking you had met her somewhere before. Her eyes kept a decorum, almost no sorrow. I glanced again at the roses sitting on the granite counter. They were white, tipped in red. Amelia reentered the room in a quick pace, the long shanks of hair trying to catch up with her body.

"Is this okay? It's a few years old but he hasn't changed."

Her last word caught in her throat. She paused and the voice was again free from outward emotion. Decorum restored. "Where do you want this placed?"

Ike took the picture from her. I studied the photograph. Grant Parkin combed his hair to the right. The gray suit was double breasted, with a striped tie tucked neatly in the collar of a white shirt. His chin was dimpled, and the left eyebrow dipped a bit lower than the right.

Amelia sat down again. I waited until Ike signaled he was ready.

"We didn't know your husband," I started. "What can you tell us about him?"

"Grant was a good husband. A hard-working person who stayed on the road a lot. He loved his job because of what it meant to people."

"Meant?"

"He didn't sell directly to the public, but Grant made sure the finest diamonds made it to his customers. Diamonds meant for young couples, or as a gift. He took his job as a courier seriously."

She took her right hand and pushed her fingers through the dark strands. "I just want justice. Grant was going to meet someone. I don't know who it was or why, but I want justice. I can tell you he was meeting regular with that person and they were working on a project. He kept telling me it was going to be big."

Sandra Capers leaned forward. "He never said what the project was about?"

"No. The police kept asking me. We went through all kinds of records, but nothing."

Capers had a follow-up. "Did your husband know Cole Walker?"

Amelia Parkin placed her hands in her lap. Her right foot started to tap a slow beat. "I can't get into that. I just can't say right now." Her eyes wandered from one camera to the next. "I just want everyone to keep Grant in their thoughts. That's all I have to say."

She stood. This time it took all her strength to pull her body to a standing position. The photographers started breaking down the equipment, collapsing the legs of their tripods. I whispered a question in Amelia's direction.

"Where is your husband's car?"

"Right out front. It hasn't been moved."

"So, someone picked him up?"

"Yes. I told the police I was asleep at the time. I don't even think I heard him leave."

"And your husband never mentioned a Cole Walker?"

"Not that I can think of . . ."

She walked us to the door, past the picture of Grant Parkin, past the rose-scented air of the kitchen. We stood outside adjusting to the breeze kicking up from the north. I noticed a business card on a coffee table. The name said Frank Tower, Insurance Investigator. I wrote the name in my pad. Just before she closed the door, she stopped; her eyes brightened as if an important thought locked into place.

"I don't want to put the spotlight on someone who is perfectly innocent, but my husband spent a lot of time recently with . . ." she paused. "Come to think of it, I only remember a nickname. Nothing else. Grant called him The Maker."

Chapter 18

"What are you thinking?" It seemed Ike waited for me to answer rather than watch the road. I glanced at the windshield and the backs of cars, then back to Ike.

"Don't kill us," I said, staring at the steering wheel. "But I guess we're in a race." Ike's van sped up. He kept me from concentrating on trying to figure out Grant Parkin's final moments.

"Race?" Ike veered into another lane.

"Who can find The Maker first, me or Capers?"

The van crossed Lombart Avenue. Ike turned into the strip mall and parked in front of the Diamond Escape, Ltd. Through the wall of glass, I counted four customers. I went in ahead of Ike. Under the track lights, the gems were glowing. There were trays of sparklers. I tried to remember the names and shapes from conversations with Cat. On one side, blue topaz rings shined to a brilliance. The diamonds came in all kinds of shapes. Round cuts, princess, emerald, oval, pear, marquise, and trillion.

"There are a lot of myths and legends when it comes to

diamonds." Dobb surprised me. His voice boomed in the small environs of the shop.

"Legends and myths?" I said.

"Of course."

Ike stepped into the shop, trying to keep his tripod from hitting any of the glass cases.

Dobb pulled out a key, which was connected to a long metal chain. He opened a lock on a case and guided his hand over the trays of jewels. Two other customers stopped their search to watch Dobb. He pulled out a diamond from a display box and pulled it toward him. He took out a green pad and placed the gem in the middle of the square.

"As you probably know, this is a princess cut. One of my favorites." He cleared his throat. "Legend has it, going into battle, great warriors would cover their breastplates with diamonds to make their enemies bow down."

"Did it work?"

"Sometimes. It's also been said that centuries ago, they ate diamonds thinking they could cure illness. Today I just want people to enjoy them." He lowered his voice. "I see you got my message."

"Where can we do the interview?"

"Back here."

We followed him to the tiny room in the back. I adjusted my sight to the dark hallway. "Listen," I began. "Have you ever heard of someone with a nickname of The Maker?"

"The Maker . . . hmmm." I heard him hum the question like a song, carrying the words with a low sustained grunt, stepping around a desk. The humming stopped. "I'm not aware of anyone by that name, but if something comes up, I'll give you a call. How's that?"

Ike squeezed into an area not much bigger than the size of a throw rug. "Hope you don't mind it back here, but I didn't want to say anything in front of the customers."

"No problem," I told him.

Ike had the gear set up in minutes, and I asked the first question. "You saw the diamonds owned by Cole Walker. What is it about them that got your interest?"

"I don't know how to say this any other way, but I would really like to see them again. They need to be examined on a closer level, but . . ." He folded, then unfolded his arms. His eyes no longer looked at me, but instead focused on an imaginary object on the table.

"I've never seen diamonds like that. I mean, no flaws, something beyond what I have encountered. I just want to examine them one more time."

His gaze again centered on my face. "There could be an explanation. There is the chance, just a chance that they might be . . ." He stopped. I asked him the same question three more times, but he did not give me an answer.

Chapter 19

I made it back to the news station with my head full of questions. Who was The Maker, and what was the connection to Cole Walker? The specialty of Morgan's diamonds intrigued me. How did Grant Parkin end up in Cole's car? What happened to the missing diamonds? I gave up on trying to connect everything—for now.

My story was assigned to the 5 P.M. newscast. I went over my elements: the search of Cole Walker's home, the news conference with police, an interview with Parkin's widow, and the short sound clip with the jeweler. I blocked out the story in my mind and starting typing. The strongest element I had was the interview with Amelia Parkin, so I started the story there and moved to the search of Cole's house, then an interview with police. I figured I wasn't over on my time allotment, so I included a sound byte with Dobb.

Mike Brendon was corralled into a corner section of his desk, eyes peering into the computer, as if hiding something. I looked over his shoulder and he slid a doctor's appointment slip across the table in my direction. "The unknown sometimes makes it tough," he told me. "I've been on a few Web sites studying this." Brendon tucked the piece of paper in his shirt pocket. "If it goes down I have diabetes, I'll just take my meds, do my shots, and keep going."

"It's going to take more than that to pull you off that desk."

Brendon nodded. On his computer screen was a Web site about diabetes. "There's a lot of information."

He cleared the computer screen and tapped his keypad until a rundown of the newscasts appeared. "I'm a slow-moving train wreck when it comes to doctors." He fingered some more keys, hitting them hard, like the days of banging letters on a typewriter. "I won't see'm unless I'm forced."

I was about to ask Brendon who made him get checked for diabetes but he just stared at the computer. A deadline loomed so I directed my attention back on the script. Once the script was approved by an upper-level producer, Ike needed just forty minutes to edit the package. Immediately after the taped story aired, the director punched up a shot of me sitting before Ike's camera in the newsroom. I gave a thirty second live wrap-up in the studio and prepared to leave. The phone on my desk rang.

"Hello."

"So, I have to call you to finally catch up to you." Cat's voice took me to a place of solitude.

"I'm about to leave."

"Don't go to my place. Meet me at G.G.'s Garden."

Traffic was an easy ride and I made it there in half an hour. G.G.'s Garden was a plant nursery in the western end of Broward county, owned by her friend G.G. Everson.

Just to the west of the nursery, the Florida Everglades. The place was on the fringe of the county. G.G. considered poisonous cottonmouth snakes and raccoons all backyard friends. I arrived just as the sun emblazoned the horizon in red-purple clouds.

I parked near Cat's van. A twenty-foot tall red bougainvillea stood to one side, as a landmark, covering a shadow-box fence.

G.G. kept everything grouped by size. Smaller plants of foxtails and mondo grass were kept up front. Tall palms took up the back row. Before he died, G.G.'s father built a wooden building to serve as a cashier stand and shop. A motor recycled water, sending a flow trickling over interlocking rocks, into a shallow pool full of koi.

"Hi Matt." Cat Miller stepped from the heart of the shop with a hibiscus flower stuck in her hair and smelled of gardenia. She could have been an island princess. As she walked toward me, she adjusted the flower so it wouldn't fall.

"I like the look." I stepped closer, kissing her cheek. Her neck had a sheen of sweat and the tips of her nails were encrusted with dirt.

"The kids are in the back doing homework. G.G. has an air-conditioned area where you can eat over here." Cat's hand pointed in the direction of the shop. "And the kids can't wait for Friday."

The sun was gone now. Rising from the floor of the Glades, the sky was a wall of black mist.

"Are you helping G.G.?" I asked.

"Why don't you come inside for a moment. I have something to tell you."

On the ground, the entire complex was covered in crushed rock. Cat turned around just once, giving me a wink before mounting the stairs to the wooden deck. The only light in the room came from a small lamp behind the counter. I joined Cat at a bench off to one side. A strong breeze bent the tops of the queen palms. I repeated my question. "Does G.G. need your help?"

"Matt, I'm quitting my job next week."

"Why? I thought you liked it at the bank?"

"I found something better. It's something I want to do."

Cat leaned back against the cushion of the bench. The lamp warmed one side of her face in hues of brown. Her eyes stayed focused on me, burning through the darkness. She let out a long sigh. "I've been thinking about this for some time now. I'm going to be working here full time."

"Here, meaning the nursery?"

"Is that so hard to imagine?"

"No. I know you've been out here a lot but . . ."

Cat moved closer, not stopping until we almost shared the same breath. I felt a surge from within me, firing nerve endings and impulses, causing a bump in my heart rate. She kept coming at me, letting our lips touch. I stayed there, pushing closer, drifting into a long kiss. Her fingers stretched over the top of mine until she held my hands firmly in hers. Cat eased back, moving from shadow to light, finally resting her shoulders against the bench.

"I'm not just some person helping G.G. I took some of the money my mother left me and I bought into this place. I'm a part owner now."

"That's fast. I think it's fantastic."

"Well, all the paperwork still has to be worked out and

signed and it won't be final for a few weeks, but I agreed in principal this morning." Cat paused as if waiting for me to answer.

"When will all this start?"

"Today. Now. We never had a chance to talk about this. Before I made my final decision, I wanted to speak to you last night but you had to run out on a story. I just didn't want to wait any longer." She paused. The light flickered against her skin. "I kept trying to reach you last night, but you were out with . . . what's her name?"

"Morgan."

"Yes. I really wanted us to discuss this, but you never seemed to have the time."

"I'm sorry. Had to work the story. I think this is a great idea."

"Matt, I don't know how to say this but . . ." Her eyes dipped for only a moment before the gleam of hazel locked on me again. "Sometimes it's really important for us to talk. Important for you to make some time. Do you understand what I'm getting at?"

"I understand. And you're right."

I looked around the grounds. The plants were draped in shadow. I couldn't make out where my car was parked. The occasional chirp of crickets echoed off the back line of potted trees.

"Are you going to change the name of the place?"

"It's been G.G.'s Garden for so long, we decided not to change it now. We've got employees, a landscaping business, and we rent plants out to businesses in Fort Lauderdale."

"Rent?"

"Sure. What business has time to mess with a ten-foot

tall Rhapis Palm? We take care of them, switch them out, whatever."

There was a new level of enthusiasm in her voice. Cat smiled as she spoke.

"And Jason and Shauna?"

"That's the best part. I set my own hours. If I need to pick them up at school, then I go get them."

I ran out of questions.

A low-pitched voice came at us from the steps. "And she's got some great ideas about getting more customers in here." G.G. Everson was a tall woman. Lines of corn-rowed hair curved back down the slope of her head. The tips of her nails were also rimmed in dirt.

"You're not trying to talk her out of this, are you?" G.G. laughed with a certain heartiness. She wore a denim blouse with a few buttons open, and jeans. Her brown eyes matched the tone of her skin.

"I'm applauding her," I said.

"Good, cause it's already settled." G.G. let out a guttural laugh, her eyes glowing in the dim light.

"All right," I said. "Let me ask the questions I would have asked last night." I looked around the property. "You two going to be okay out without . . ."

"Men?" G.G. completed my sentence. "My husband asked the same thing, but I've done okay so far, and believe me, you don't want to mess with me." She patted her chest three times and let out another laugh.

Cat said, "She's got a security system tied in with the police and an emergency button. And there's the employees."

"No security cameras?"

"Not yet," G.G. said. "But they're in the plans. We're getting them soon."

"Okay. And the financials?"

G.G.'s chest rose with her sigh as though this was a speech she gave more than once in the past few days. "I'm solid. When my father died, I used insurance money to pay off his house, then I sold it. I've got a place not too far from here. And the overhead here isn't too bad. There's some insurance costs, two trucks, a van, and eight full-time employees. And yes, I cover their insurance."

"I checked it all out." Cat stood off to my left.

"It sounds like you have it all covered. It's just that the nearest police shop is a few miles from here, and then there's nothing." I pointed west, to the lightening cells developing in the Everglades. White jagged lines scratched the sky, followed by thunder.

"I've been here seven years by myself and the crew. With Cat here, we can devote more time to landscaping and bid city contracts. That's her end of it." G.G. pulled her car keys from a rear pocket on her jeans.

"Mom, my homework is done." Shauna shouted across the grounds, her head leaned out of the door of a trailer.

Cat cupped her hands. "We're leaving. Get ready."

The door to the trailer closed and two youngsters walked toward us. "I'm tired." Cat let her hands ride down the top of her jeans, in a motion to stand up.

"Get used to it. You're a business owner. Tired is part of the deal," G.G. said.

My cell phone pulsed with a steady rhythm against my side. I hit the call button and recognized Mike Brendon's voice.

"What's up?" I asked.

Mike said, "I'm not going to try to send you out somewhere. I did that last night, but I wanted to give you some advance notice about this. And you can work on it in the morning."

"Work on what?"

"Cole Walker has disappeared from the hospital."

Chapter 20

J anet Perry opened her door a bit wider, then stepped out into the cool of a January morning in Florida. "I don't know that much," she said. Her gaze drifted to the front of Cole Walker's home.

"Anything you can tell me is appreciated." I turned the top of my pad to a clean sheet of paper. "How long have you known Cole?"

"Five years. Since I moved here. I just want him to be safe. I'm worried about him." She blinked long enough for tug lines to pull at the corners of her eyes. Ike moved the camera on his shoulder until it appeared he was comfortable. He nodded. I posed the first on-camera question.

"Did you notice anything at the Cole home last night?"

"Well, I did see the lights on in the house, but I didn't think anything about it at first. But I remembered Morgan hasn't been home. I just figured she came home again. Then this morning the car was gone."

"Did you see Morgan or Cole?"

"No. Just the lights on. I know he was wounded. I didn't know he left the hospital until I saw the news this morning. I just hope that he's okay. They are such nice people."

Janet drew fingers up to her face, her right hand stayed propped against her jaw as if to support her head.

"So you didn't see anyone leave?"

"No."

"When was the last time you talked with either of them?"

Her eyes rolled upward toward the cover of blue sky then back to my face. "He seemed like everything was going right in the world. No worries—until this." Her voice dropped.

My pause let Ike know the interview was over. I thanked her for her time and walked with Ike to the front of Cole's house. Cole's early exit from the hospital made him look suspicious in the death of the courier. I made the perfunctory knock on the door, but there was no answer. The house was quiet. I stepped back off the property and studied the surroundings. The mailbox, mounted on the wall next to the door, appeared empty. I figured the police probably had the place on a surveillance watch, along with checking recent phone records, incoming calls to the hospital, and in-hospital camera surveillance tapes. They might also monitor Morgan's credit card, incoming and outgoing numbers to their cell phones, and bank withdrawals.

I called Morgan's cell phone and left a message. "Okay, Ike, where is he?"

Ike stepped away from the camera which was resting on the tripod. "I'm trying to figure out: Is he running from someone or is he running to something?"

"Well, think about it. He's shot in the shoulder, but it's a through-and-through wound and he's healing. He just can't move around too much or he'll tear up his stitching. It's obvious, Morgan or someone helped him out of the hospital. Or was he taken out? Morgan saw someone the other night. The person who shot him might be after him. That could be why he skipped."

My instructions from Mike Brendon were clear. If I could scrape together enough information, I would be in the noon newscast. Otherwise, they would leave me alone to look for Cole. I had an interview with the neighbor, and police were still deciding if they wanted to comment. It wasn't much.

My cell phone vibrated with the number to the newsroom. I called Brendon.

"Check this out," he said.

"Something new on Cole?"

"No, but the widow Parkin called you. She wanted you to know that she checked some records from her husband to find out who he's been working for lately."

"And?"

"She found a recent pay stub for L.M. Cornerstone Enterprises."

The front door to L.M. Cornerstone Enterprises opened to a room of dingy carpets and dime-store artwork on the walls. A sign was mounted above one office door, its huge lettering covered an entire wall to get in all the letters for Cornerstone. The sign was faded white and the tips of all four corners turned inward.

"Who let you in here?" The secretary adjusted her glasses, her eyes made larger by the thick lenses.

"I'm Matt Bowens from Channel 14. Is Roland Campton in?"

"He's busy at the moment. What did you say your name was?"

"Bowens. Matt Bowens." I kept my voice low and controlled, responding to her nervous reaction when she saw me.

"Wait right here." I watched her give a light tap to the door below the huge company sign, then she stepped inside. A few moments of mumbled conversation ended with her walking into the room, followed by a heavyset man wearing a pinky ring, mounted with diamonds.

"Can I help you?" His voice had the calm, rounded edge of someone used to dealing with crises.

"I'm Matt Bowens. This is Ike Cashing. I'm here to ask you about Cole Walker. He was found shot and bleeding at a warehouse owned by you. I just thought you could help us figure out what Cole was doing there? Is that okay?"

He stared at the camera. "Sure. Ask your questions."

I raised the microphone. "Like I said, any idea on why Cole Walker was found at your warehouse?"

"Mr. Bowens, I would be pleased to address your concerns on any other day, but I'm right in the middle of something and I can't squeeze you into what is already a very busy schedule."

"How long did Grant Parkin work for you?"

"Who?"

"Grant Parkin. Diamond courier. He was found dead in the front seat of an SUV over at the Clarkston Hotel. How long did he work for you?"

A smile formed on his face. "Any connections I had with him are private."

"Then there's the matter of the missing diamonds. Would you know anything about that?"

"You know, I change my mind about the interview." His eyes flickered between me and Ike.

"What was Cole Walker doing at your warehouse?"

"Get out. Now." As he spoke, he raised his left arm up and thrust a hand into the lens of Ike's camera. Five beefy fingers and a palm the size of a baseball mitt swung at Ike until he backed up. I stepped in front of the bulky form, letting him come into me rather than Ike.

"We're leaving," I shouted. "What did Cole do for you?" We were a collection of arms and bodies, twisting and jousting toward the door. His pinky ring got caught in the rubber camera lens housing. I kept shouting the questions at Campton. The door slammed against the jam. I heard the lock mechanism turn hard in the frame. I studied Ike to see if he was okay. My biggest concern was a hand pushing the camera lens into a photographer's eye.

"I'm fine." Ike stepped back from the front door and took a few video shots of the office building.

I didn't see the Porsche at first. The shine of the yellow Carrara caught reflections from the sun until the car moved under the shade of a black olive tree. Two men were inside. The passenger was black. The driver, white. His right arm reached up to adjust the sunglasses. I thought the driver had a tattoo. His blond hair was streaked with darker strands. I turned to them, looking to confirm my suspicions about the tattoo.

"We've got guests." I said.

Ike turned from the building, leaning his head from the eyepiece.

"Nice car."

The Porsche backed up, moving far down the street before the driver turned and made a left, picking up speed, the tires tossing off rocks and making leaves swirl in its wake. I couldn't catch the tag.

"Maybe they were coming to see Campton and we scared them off?" I pulled at the top of the writer's pad.

Chapter 21

"It's not a crime to leave the hospital early." Patrick O'Donnell eyed the microphone as if to make sure it wasn't on. "We still need to find him though because he's a material witness in his own shooting, but he can't be charged with skipping the hospital. Stupidity maybe, but nothing else. I can't say that on camera, but that's how I feel." We stood outside the police station. O'Donnell's arms were locked against his chest.

A man emerged through the front doors, arguing to himself about a police report. O'Donnell said he couldn't update the murder investigation or Cole's shooting. No suspects. Nothing.

"Maybe tomorrow," he said.

I stood in the back parking lot of the news building, atop the seawall, watching a school of tarpon stay fixed in one position, their silver scales shining like polished steel through the glimmer of the waves. A line of boats cruised past buoy markers, headed through the cut toward deeper water. I heard Ike Cashing long before he reached me, the dangle of keys banged against his belt with each step.

"What would make Cole leave the hospital early? Scared of someone?" I asked.

"You've got one dead in Cole's car, a trashed home, and the shooter on the loose." Ike squinted at the sun.

"Maybe it's something else," I said. The lead tarpon jutted forward, cutting off the path of a small fish, opening his jaw to take it in, then moved back into place. "I checked the video when we got back and went over statements. The night at the Clarkston Hotel, did you see Cole's camera?"

Ike's face turned into a reflective collection of turned down eyebrows and the clenched teeth made his jaw bulge.

"I don't remember seeing it. And it wasn't at the warehouse. Police didn't find it at the house."

"Maybe our suspects weren't looking for diamonds at Cole's house. Maybe the prize was a videotape shot by Cole? Something with evidence on it."

"But where?" Ike said.

"If Morgan helped him out of the hospital, they might have her on surveillance video. But the first thing Cole might do is get to his camera gear and the video. Did Cole ever mention a storage place he used?"

"Mostly he used his garage. But there was a time he kept some big stuff at Borker's Storage over on Hollywood Boulevard."

"Big place?"

"He had a huge jib and some other stuff." Ike's arms were stretched wide. The jib was a giant handworked crane to mount the camera for smooth high angle shots.

"Think about it though. Photographers are not going to be too far from their camera."

"The night he was shot, he probably arrived with it." Ike dragged his hands through his hair.

"If he thought there was going to be trouble, why wouldn't he stash the camera somewhere quick, to pick it up later? I mean, the first place they would check is his car."

"You want to go by the warehouse?" Ike asked.

"We've got some time."

On the way I called the producers in Miami to give them a rundown of what I had so far: the interview with Cole's neighbor, an update on Cole's disappearance, the confrontation at Cornerstone Enterprises and the connection to murder victim Grant Parkin. The vision of Campton's pinky ring in my face was still fresh on my mind. For now I was given the lead of the 5:30 newscast. If I got anything stronger, I would be moved up to the 5:00.

We found the front of the unit was still marked with yellow crime tape. We walked up close. The doorknob was covered with a red plastic seal, warning the public not to enter. I looked around. The familiar plume of wood dust curled up from the entrance to the woodshop, three stalls down. I entered first.

"Mr. Stafford, I believe?" I motioned for Ike to put his camera down.

"You back?"

"No camera this time, but I have a few more questions, if you don't mind."

"It's your time." He wiped back a line of sweat from his brow, his eyes steady on a plank of wood. The saw was silent for the moment.

"Have you seen anything strange?"

"Strange?"

"Maybe some people looking for something? Or a Porsche."

"The Porsche isn't strange." His eyes never came up to meet mine. He kept his concentration on the wood, getting the piece lined up exactly for the cutting blade.

"You're right. I'm not sure what I'm looking for."

"Well, there is one thing."

He glanced up for the first time. "My neighbor over here tells me a woman was going through the garbage at the end of the complex. By the way he described it, she was dressed too nice to be Dumpster diving."

"Where's the Dumpster?"

"Right when you first come in the complex. You can't miss it."

"When?"

"Not too long ago," he said.

"When's garbage pickup day?"

"Tomorrow."

I shouted a thank you. Outside his door, the Dumpster wasn't in sight. Ike gripped the camera by its handle, but he could not keep up with me. I ran the length of the stalls. From each work station, eyes followed me, probably wondering why a man dressed in a tie was running the stretch of the parking lot. The Dumpster was nestled up alongside the building, a stench hung in the air. I opened the heavy lid and found discarded fast food wrappers and the gathered waste from the warehouse.

A car moved past me, just close enough for me to see Morgan driving by in a slate Mustang, the car picking up speed, her hair blowing in the gust. Next to her sat Cole

Walker. His head was tilted back, almost oblivious to what was happening. I guessed he must be on some kind of strong pain medication. The car was moving faster, but I was close enough to extend my microphone. Ike aimed his camera.

"Why did you leave the hospital?" I yelled.

Cole was slumped back in the seat and he looked at me.

I yelled again, "Cole, why did you leave the hospital? Who shot you?"

He just looked at me. I kept running alongside the car. Then, in almost a mumble, "You won't understand," Cole said.

Morgan's eyes flashed at me for only a moment, long enough for her car to push into the main street and away from the cluster of shops. Then they were gone. Ike stopped a few feet from me, propped the camera on his shoulder, aimed at the car and clicked the controls. The car joined the traffic, and Ike stayed on them until Morgan was no longer in sight.

"Well, we got a bit. Not much but something," he said. "Find anything?"

I looked down into the Dumpster. "If they came for the camera, I think they got it."

I called Miami. After telling about the new video of Morgan and a quick sound pop of Cole, they moved me into the 5 P.M. newscast.

Chapter 22

Dobb stood before me, massaging his chin with his left hand. "I'm not sure I understand your question." Behind him, rows of gems sparkled under the room lights.

"It's just that you expressed so much interest in Morgan's diamonds, you wanted to see them again." I looked at my watch. A deadline was looming.

"I just wanted to justify something in my mind about them, that's all," he said.

"Justify?"

"I thought I saw the same clarity in a similar diamond, but I needed another look."

Ike jammed his hands into his pockets. His camera was in the car and he leaned against the door jamb as if he didn't know what to do without his gear.

"There is one connection through all of this," I started. "From Cole's disappearance to Grant Parkin's murder." I watched his face, gauged his movement. "The connection is the diamonds."

"Are you sure? It could be a coincidence," Dobb said in a low voice.

"I don't think so. The death of a diamond courier, who just happened to work at times for the very owner of the warehouse where Cole was shot. I'm here to see what you make out of all this."

Dobb pressed his lips into a broken line, while a customer brushed past him, moving from one glass display to the rows of watches on the other side of the room.

Dobb said, "I don't want to upset my customers, all this talk of murder."

"You want to go outside?"

"No. I don't have a lot to add to what you said. I can't imagine why . . . what's the victim's name?"

"Grant Parkin."

"I don't see what Mr. Parkin would be doing with your friend the photographer. I offer my assistance if you come up with more information."

"How long have you known Cole and Morgan?"

"Not long. Besides the ring, I sold them a bracelet a year ago. Morgan liked how I treated them."

Another customer entered the store. The soft door ring echoed a hollow sound in the small room. Dobb glanced at the faces, probably wondering if he would lose a sale while he was preoccupied with me.

"What a day," Ike said to the open room. He flicked his eyes between two television monitors. One monitor showed video from the tape we shot during the past seven hours, the other monitor showed a finished news story, complete with my voice track, Ike's pictures, and the short interview with Cole Walker. The station played it up as the first interview since he got shot. I kept asking myself what he meant by I wouldn't understand.

Twenty minutes later I stood in the small studio and relayed the facts before a live camera. I hoped Channel 14 would let me stay on the story one more day. I drove home, checked my e-mails, voicemail messages, and a stack of letters in the bin. Cat called an hour later and we stayed on the phone until the late news came on. I prepared myself for a new story in the morning.

Chapter 23

The sun wouldn't make an impression for at least another hour. Mike Brendon called me at 6 A.M. and said someone called police about a body found in the Everglades. I drove the expressway to meet Ike at a truck stop along U.S. 27, twenty miles west of Fort Lauderdale. Most car traffic was headed in the other direction. There were no homes in the Glades, just miles of protected marsh where the Florida panther roamed, and alligators floated down canals dotted with hyacinth.

The truck stop was a popular location, but I had a hard time finding the place since the entire county was shrouded in fog. I parked, got into Ike's van, and we drove south. Ike kept the van well under the speed limit. Our van poked a hole in the thick white air until we reached a police command post two miles away. A uniformed officer wearing orange gloves directed us to a clearing near the road, where Ike parked. I briefly saw the gun and shoulder patch of a uniform yards away. Stalks of moist grass brushed my shoes with each step until we reached him. We waited.

106

The sky and ground blended into a sheet of gray mist. The rolls of clouds hugged the ground, hiding melaleuca trunks, and wild cocoplum, exposing only the tips of a few palmetto palms. Twisted branches rose up out of the fog. A hint of a morning breeze was coming off the Glades, and I watched the fog take shapes as irregular as ghosts.

Through the mist, I saw it.

A hand protruded up through the boggy air, the fingers extended upward to the sky as if to warn us to stay away. A gust pushed out of the west, blowing past us. The wisps of gray fog curled around the dead fingers and broke off into tight circles.

"Man, this is eerie." Ike kept his camera on his shoulder, the lens dark, staring in the distance. News policy didn't allow uncovered bodies on television.

I surveyed what I could. Past experience told me a canal should be thirty feet away. No car for the victim. If he was dumped here, the crime techs might find footprints. I've been to this area before. Once three tourists got lost in their rented airboat. They were spotted by a helicopter pilot on a return flight from Key Largo.

This was the same locale where a fisherman called 911 after he reached into the dark water and was bitten by a cottonmouth. They got him to a hospital before he collapsed. I admired the beauty of the Glades, but a person had to respect the notion of being thrown into danger by slipping off the bank into alligator-infested water.

The sun was struggling to burn through the fog. The outline of a tree canopy, bleached in twilight, served as a horizon. The form of a unmarked detective's car pulled up next to our van. I guessed they couldn't process the scene in the current conditions and risk stepping on crucial evidence. We stood there, uniforms, detectives, reporters, and photographers, all watching shapes appear then fade into the crystal bog.

I turned, looking for O'Donnell. Nothing. I walked back to the car and found detective Victor leaning against his car. His face was just a round faded image until I moved closer. Behind us, cars passed in a slow procession because of the weather and the rubber-necking draw of curiosity.

"What do you have?" I asked him.

"Not much. We're not going to contaminate a crime scene. We'll be out there soon enough, then we'll know."

"How did you find out about the body?"

"A phone call. Someone tipped 911. A very short conversation."

"Male voice, or female?"

"Can't release that yet."

"Are you sure this is a homicide?"

"We're *not* sure. Paramedics have been out there. Fire rescue did the check. He's gone. Now we have to fill in the details."

I nodded and walked the length of cars back to Ike Cashing. I heard movement in the branches and sensed a stirring in the canal, a hawk getting ready for a hunt, mullet stripping algae from tall lengths of giant grass.

We spoke very little as if the fog robbed our vocal chords and made us stand silent. The presence of the body left us staring off at times rather than face the prone man several yards away.

Twenty minutes passed and fingers of sunlight finally cut through the fog, exposing green forms of trees and mounds of dollar weed. The body was still uncovered, forcing Ike to leave his camera off. A shaft of light revealed more of the hand and arm.

"Do you see that?" I pointed to the gnarled fingers and the shirtless arm. Ike's glance was now fixed on the figure.

"I don't believe it," he said.

Just inches down on the arm, I could make out the outlined tattoo of a knife. We couldn't be sure until we saw the face. The figure on the ground was the driver of the Porsche that followed us.

Chapter 24

"You sure it's the same person?" Ike almost let the camera slip out of his hands. He grabbed the rectangular housing in a quick motion, as if his next breath depended on saving the camera. "This fog makes everything slippery."

"I need a closer look or a look through that lens," I said, stepping toward Ike.

Ike set up the camera on the tripod and zoomed in closer.

"There," he said. "It's all yours."

I leaned into the view finder. The face was angled directly at the sun. The tattoo was the same one I remembered. The hair color matched.

"So, where's his Porsche?" I said, pulling back from the camera.

"He was dumped, so who knows where he left his car. And don't forget he had a friend."

Over my shoulder, a uniform was doing his best to get traffic to move along. He kept waving his arms, trying to lock eyes with an idle driver and keep cars moving down U.S. 27. Two crime scene techs walked a few feet in the direction of the body and then stopped. One bent down, moved a still camera into place and fired off a shot. Then another. A small plastic cone was placed by something on the ground. Then a third and fourth photograph were taken.

They continued the process until they reached the body. Several minutes later, after checking the figure, one tech opened a tarp and covered him. Ike started photographing the scene.

The fog was gone and the area was awash in sunshine. Slight ripples creased the top of the canal water. The body was much closer to the bank than I realized. His feet were pointed south, his head north. His eyes were open.

"He couldn't have been here that long." I inched a few steps closer.

Every few minutes, a tech would motion to a detective and the tarp was adjusted so the tech could continue working. More photographs were made. They checked his pockets and looked at his nails.

One hour passed. I gave Mike a call, and he said we were a live story on the noon newscast. I felt a tap on my right shoulder and looked back to see O'Donnell with a clipboard.

"I've got some information for you." As he spoke he looked around, probably checking for other reporters.

"What's up?" I turned into the sun.

"We think we can identify him by noon."

"He's a regular?"

"If you mean regular as in arrested before, then yes, we know who he is." O'Donnell took the clipboard and put it behind his back.

"So what's his story?," I asked.

"He's been a guest of our state prison twice before. He did two hits in Raiford after getting popped for bank robbery and high stakes burglaries."

"Meaning?"

"He was a condo climber, going up several stories to take jewelry and diamonds. High end stuff, but mainly diamonds."

"So what's he doing out here waiting for the gators?"

"We'd love to find out."

"Was he wanted for anything?"

"Right now, nothing. Clean as far as we know. He checked in with his parole officer, did everything by the book. Then this."

O'Donnell looked beyond me at the body. The figure was a few feet from a section of tasseled wild grass.

"You got a name on him?"

"I do but I can't give it to you yet. Give me about thirty minutes."

"I think this is the same guy who was following us yesterday."

"This guy?" O'Donnell's thumb poked the air in the direction of the figure on the ground.

"I'm not a hundred percent sure, but I think it's him. I hate to put it this way, but it was real quick. Ike saw him too."

"What were you doing to get this guy following you?"

"Nothing. Just tracking a story. But he had someone with him."

A Channel 14 live truck pulled in at the end of the line of police cars. A minute after stopping, the tall metal microwave mast pushed up out of the top of the truck.

"I remember when he was busted the last time."

O'Donnell kicked a coral rock with his toe. "The funny thing about this is he's been clean for years. I mean model citizen clean."

"An unpaid debt, maybe?" I watched Ike leave us, heading down the roadway.

"As far as I know, he never rolled on anyone. He swore he'd never be a snitch and he stayed that way. But when you run in his world, who knows." O'Donnell rubbed a growing line of sweat from his brow. "It's possible something made him come out of retirement."

"His next of kin here in south Florida?"

"No. A sister in New Jersey and that's about it. We called her right off as soon as we saw the vic."

"Where has he been living?"

O'Donnell checked his notes. "Over on Loketon Park Boulevard. I'll give you the exact address in a few minutes. You say he was following you?"

"It's possible." It was enough information for O'Donnell. Ike set up his tripod some fifty feet away. Crews from four television stations were kept from the crime scene by the guard rail and a uniform.

"By the way." I waited until O'Donnell took his gaze from the canal. "The diamonds from the courier murder, did they ever turn up?"

"No."

"And are you planning a search of this guy's house?"

"As soon as the warrant is signed."

The van arrived to pick up the body fifteen minutes before the newscast. Ike recorded the video and we tacked it on the end of the edited story. O'Donnell briefed Sandra Capers, myself, newspaper, and radio reporters. Police would only say he was shot to death and gave us a name. Eric Lopell was identified by O'Donnell as the victim. He had two convictions and a hung jury on a third case, which the state refused to return to trial. One more conviction and Lopell would be sentenced under the newer guidelines of a career criminal and face a long hit of up to thirty years in prison. Police told us he kept out of trouble, and stayed low-key. I did a live report for the newscast and included the information on seeing Lopell outside the office building. Then I called Mike Brendon.

"Do we have some file video on him?"

"Tons." Brendon said. "We covered his second trial almost gavel to gavel. This guy was like a fly going up walls."

Along the canal an afternoon wind stirred the long branches of an Australian pine tree. The snout, eyes, and raised back of an alligator drifted down the middle of the dark water.

Chapter 25

By 1:30, Ike's van rolled to a stop just as Sandra Capers emerged from a car. She grabbed a Channel 8 microphone, rolling the thing in her hands, like a baton in a relay. We approached the front of Lopell's house. Everything about it made me think of old Florida. All windows, back to front, were open. Flat roofs and thick walls. The place must have been eighty years old.

A uniform stood guard near the door. In four places on the jamb, red crime tape sealed the entrance until the warrant arrived.

"Left or right?" I asked Capers. She followed my gaze to the houses on either side of the rock wall.

"Left." That's the direction we'd take to knock on doors. A green SUV was parked in front the house on the left. We rang the doorbell and waited.

A woman in a business suit answered. She was almost as tall as Capers, with large brown eyes. She pressed a length of hair back behind her ear. "Can I help you? I'm late."

"We just wanted to know if you ever spoke to your neighbor?" Sandra Capers kept the microphone down at her side.

"Eric? All the time. Why?"

I looked at Capers. She released a sigh and stepped back from the front door. I sensed Capers didn't want to cross a line and tell her Lopell was dead. Releasing that kind of information led to the unknown. A person might drop, just faint away from hearing what happened. The woman studied her front yard. Two marked police cars blocked Lopell's driveway.

"What's going on? I've been inside all morning?"

"So, you haven't talked with police?" I said.

She stared at me. Finally she blinked a few times as if the whole scene was overwhelming: police in the street and two reporters with cameras at her front door. She cradled a large package in the crook of her arm, but it slipped against her body until she readjusted her fingers to get a better grip.

"Excuse me." She jammed the package against her body a second time and walked off the distance to the police cruiser, her left eye quivered. One uniform straightened up as she approached. We were too far away to hear the conversation. Her face contorted with emotion as the words washed over her. She dropped the package. The officer bent down to help pick it up. The walk back toward us was slow, her eyes aimed at the ground.

"I'm sorry," Capers began. "How long have you known him?"

She let her gaze come up slow until she met our eyes.

"Just two years, since I moved in." Her look was solemn, her words laced with anxiety.

I raised my microphone. "If it's okay, we'd like to ask you if you remember seeing him yesterday?"

"Yesterday was a blur." Her eyes stayed transfixed on

the police cars. "I had so much to do. I only saw him for a second. He was getting out of his car."

"You remember what kind of car?" I asked.

"Just a car. No wait." She paused. Her eyes came back to the cameras. "It was a fancy car. A porsche. A yellow Porsche. But for some reason, Eric wasn't driving."

"And the driver?"

"I couldn't see. Like I said, I had a lot on my mind."

Capers pulled the microphone back to her mouth and posed a question. "Any reason why anyone would want to harm him?"

"Eric? No. The entire time I knew him, I've never been inside his house. Not once."

"Did you see what happened inside the car?" I asked.

"It was so quick. I mean I had a board meeting, some errands to run. I didn't think about it."

"Did Lopell sound worried or concerned about anything?" I eased the microphone closer to her.

"I didn't know him that well. All I know is he seemed busy, or rather busier than before. It was like he was involved in something." She looked away from the microphones long enough to let us know she was finished talking.

Sandra Capers sneaked a look at the other homes. Three houses down a man was reaching for his car keys. Patience left Sandra's face. We thanked her for speaking to us and approached the man down the block but he didn't remember Lopell.

The faded navy-blue car of Detective Victor parked behind the two police units. A crime-scene bus rolled to a stop yards from Victor, the hum of internal generators replaced the quiet.

*   *   *

We crisscrossed the street and checked homeowners. Most didn't know Lopell, others were on a wave-hello-and-good-bye basis. During the next two hours, crime techs carried out marked evidence bags. During the search, I looked for any surprise on their faces, a hint of a discovery. Nothing.

Detective Victor refused our overtures to answer a question and O'Donnell never showed up.

We drove back to the office and entered the newsroom to Mike Brendon with a phone jammed up against his ear. I pulled a video file book from the shelf and culled the list of stories. It only took a quick minute before I came across the trial of Eric Lopell. There were several stories in the book. The reporter was Frank Cranston, who retired two years ago. I wrote down the numbers corresponding to marked video boxes on the shelf and continued my search.

I stacked seven videotapes on my desk. It took my computer a few minutes to boot up. I rolled over in my mind all the sweeping connections to Cole Walker: A dead courier in his car, missing diamonds, and now Lopell. I dragged my mouse pointer to Search and typed in ERIC LOPELL TRIAL. In a second, a listing of Cranston's scripts popped up on the screen. I noted twenty-seven other stories, all on Lopell, dealing with his exploits of stealing diamonds, his arrest and sentencing.

I wrote the tape box numbers on my pad. My history with Lopell consisted of just one story. Most of the work was done by Cranston.

Ike went for lunch but he was still set up to eat his food in his van and watch the Lopell house. After five minutes of searching I now had a stack of fifteen videotapes. I picked an edit booth and slipped a tape in the player deck. The story was on the trial. I hit play and listened. Cranston had an easy delivery, his voice was midlevel pitch and perfect for television. I had more than enough to choose from: shots of Eric Lopell walking into court, his hand waving off cameras; long sequences of Lopell, removing his blue suitcoat, sitting next to his attorney; diamonds spilled out of brown evidence bags in front of the jury. I also found a story by Cranston, on camera, physically showing viewers how Lopell used mountain climbing gear, special-fitted knee cups, and tight gloves to gain access to condos.

I hit a button and paused the video. One freeze-frame. August in south Florida can be so hot, only the locals are used to the swelter. In the body of his trial story, Cranston used file video of Lopell's arrest. Lopell appeared as cool as a December morning. His face was lined with a smile. He was wearing a short-sleeved shirt and walked along, grinning for the cameras until he raised his right arm. That's where I had stopped the video.

I stared at the tattooed arm.

The video showed Lopell walking into a police substation to surrender. I again picked up the video file book and checked the names of people who covered the story. Cranston was the main reporter on most stories. Next to Cranston's name, one name was repeated over and over for the photographer. The same person kept coming up as the one who shot most of the video.

Cole Walker.

Chapter 26

"It doesn't mean anything." Mike Brendon reached to stroke his beard and instead dropped both hands on his desk. He adjusted his glasses and said, "You're not giving Cole a chance." There was a tinge of anger in his voice.

"All I'm saying," I began, "is that there was plenty of time for Cole Walker to get to know Lopell. I'm sure there were times during that trial when he got away from his attorney long enough to talk with the camera off."

"And so now you're gonna connect some mighty big dots and say Cole was somehow tight with Lopell? I don't think so."

I grabbed the last stack of fries on my paper plate. "There is nothing solid to suggest anything."

Thoughts about Lopell built up in my mind. *Why would Lopell, the so-called new model citizen, be chasing me around in a Porsche?* My story was slated for the 5 P.M. newscast. I put together the elements of Lopell's body found in the Glades, with his history of crime in south Florida. We tracked down a defense attorney who gave us the angle about Lopell as the straight citizen.

Ike returned by 3:30 with video of crime techs bringing boxes out of Lopell's home. We put together the story and waited for my time cues.

I sat in the west end of the newsroom, which doubled as a studio, and talked to a live camera about Lopell. My taped portion of the story ran almost two minutes. When I finished, Mike Brendon had a look on his face that usually meant more work was needed to be done.

"What's up?" I said.

"I just got off the phone with Amelia, Grant Parkin's widow. She wants to talk."

"Talk? Sure, I can head out there tonight with Ike and—"

"She can't do it tonight. She stressed it's very important. She wants to do an interview and she will only talk to you. No other reporter. But it has to be in the morning."

"Tomorrow?"

"That's right."

"I'm supposed to be on vacation tomorrow."

Chapter 27

My shoes crunched on the bed of pebble rocks as I approached G.G.'s cashier stand. Remnants of the sunset were on the horizon, hues of crimson sorting through the trees.

I saw Cat in the doorway, a gust of wind pushed the loose strands away from her skin. She appeared caught up with the duties of running the nursery, yet there was a calm confidence that wasn't there before. The job agreed with her, and I just wanted to hold that picture of her. She turned around to catch me standing there watching her.

"Matt." There was change in Cat's expression, as if she moved from excitement to relief. The look of someone about to satisfy a child's dream of roller-coasters, cotton candy, and a trip to the haunted house.

"Hi, Cat."

Her jeans had a rip on the bottom. A dirt smear stretched from her thigh to her waist.

"Rough day?" I asked.

"Not really. We got two orders for landscaping. I've been going over sketches." She looked down at her jeans.

"And I helped with a load of areca palms. I dropped one." Her smile matched the soft glow of her eyes.

"Where are the kids?"

"In the back. They're trying to figure out the best route to take around the park to hit the most rides. I downloaded the map from the Internet. Are you packed?"

Before I could answer, G.G. Everson emerged from a grouping of fantail palms. "Yo Matt!" she yelled.

I waved. Cat grabbed my hand, leading me down a pathway of giant clay footprints, past the handpainted pots, out to a clearing, edged by rows of white hawthorn.

"See?" She looked off past plants lined on wooden planks and into the evening streaks of shadows.

"See what?"

She raised her arm and pointed an index finger at an arrangement of smaller plants surrounding a water fountain.

"It's my corner," Cat said. "G.G. felt I should take over a whole section and make it my own. I've got a few rows of salvia down front with some twisted vined hibiscus and that's some really tall Thai plants in the back."

"I know Shauna and Jason are ready for tomorrow," I said.

"Ready? Are you kidding me? That's all they've been talking about since school ended. No class tomorrow and then the weekend." She paused. "I promised to drive back Sunday night."

My gaze drifted to the ground, then back to Cat.

Her smile reduced to a look of concern. "What's wrong?"

"About tomorrow . . ."

She said, "Let me know if I made it too early to leave. I can change all that, and give you another thirty minutes or so to sleep."

"It's not that. I can't go tomorrow. It's just—"

"Why?" She cut me off. There was a tick of silence between us, then more seconds passed. Her face was a jumble of gyrations, weighing my words, probably figuring out what she would do next. "Is this is about Cole Walker?"

"Yes. I was hoping I could hand this to another reporter till Monday, but someone connected with the case wants to speak to me tomorrow. I really didn't see any way out of it."

"Did this just come up?"

"Just today."

Her shoulders sagged. "I've been through this before. My ex used to do stuff like this. We've been planning this for months."

"It's not like that," I told her.

Cat turned her back to me. I kept moving to her left until we faced each other again. "Cat, this is my job. When we first met and we got serious, I explained to you that I could be called away at any moment to cover a story. You said you were okay with that."

I heard young voices approaching. Shauna was carrying a new backpack, the denim was covered in logos from the amusement park. Jason followed. He tugged on his pants. Both smiled when they reached me.

Cat said, "I've got some bad news. Tomorrow's trip planned for four will now include just three. Matt has to work." She paused.

Shauna spoke up first, staring directly at me. "Why can't you go? We've been getting ready for a long time."

"I'm sorry, Shauna. I have to work tomorrow."

Jason picked an imaginary bug from his hair. "But we . . ." He ran out of breath, stopped, took in a chest full of air, and continued. "But we can still go, right?"

Cat pulled him into her, hugging the six-year old, his face pressed flat against her jeans. Shauna looked up at me, anger burned into her hazel eyes. "Do you break promises?"

"Not unless I can't help it, I'll never break a promise. But this has to do with my job and I have to go into work tomorrow. There will be another trip."

"Promise?"

"Promise."

Jason untangled himself from Cat's arms.

"Let's go home," she said. One nanosecond after Cat spoke, Jason broke into a hard run in the direction of the car. Shauna walked a pace faster than mine. Cat slowed down to match my steps.

"We're not doing too well, are we?" she said.

"We just need some time. Right now my time is tied to this story. I'm sorry."

G.G. was busy closing one of the two front gates. "Don't worry, I'll lock up," she yelled.

I wanted to pick up my cell phone and tell Brendon to forget about tomorrow, that I made plans and did not want to break them. But I couldn't leave the story. I edged closer to Cat. We walked in silence. Jason was pulling at her car door when we reached her Honda.

"Stop, Jason. You'll set off the alarm." Jason kept

pulling. Cat let Jason and Shauna inside the car. I wasn't sure if she would let me kiss her. I waited for some lead from Cat.

"We're stopping for something to eat," she started. "And then I'm going to take a shower and finish packing. Call me later if you want."

I leaned toward her but stopped in time before the car door came swinging in my direction. Cat drove east, headed for University Drive. Only Jason turned back, his face pressed against the side window.

Chapter 28

"Thank you for coming, Mr. Bowens." Amelia Parkin waved us toward the family room. "I'm sorry for the mess, but with the funeral and all, a lot of relatives have been here."

"It's okay." I assured her. Ike set up his tripod in the same place as before. I glanced in the direction of the kitchen. The roses were still there, the stems slumped over in the vase, the petals faded and piling up on the countertop.

She noticed my gaze. "I couldn't throw them away." She took a step toward the vase then stopped. "It was the last thing he gave me."

Ike broke the moment by snapping his camera into place in the tripod. He held the tiny microphone ready to clip it on the collar of her blouse.

"Before we start, you're probably wondering why I called you back?"

"Yes, I was curious."

"Please, off camera first." She positioned herself in the

chair. "Ever since this happened, I've been hounded by this . . . this investigator."

"From the police?"

"No. From the insurance company. The diamonds were insured and before they pay, this investigator is really giving me a hard time."

"He's trying to connect your husband in all of this?"

"Yes." She took both hands and swept them through her long hair. "They think the missing diamonds was an inside job, like he had something to do with his own murder. Why can't they understand?" Her hands were waving at the air.

"Let me ask you about that." I motioned to Ike and repeated my question, this time with the camera going. "What is it that concerns you about the diamonds investigation?"

"They are talking like my husband had something to do with the diamonds being stolen. I am here to tell you there is no truth to that." Her right hand covered her left, gripping down so hard, her veins bore rigid lines down her hands and arm. "My husband died a terrible death and someone out there knows the truth about why he had to die." She paused, as if to think about what she was about to say. "I think I know why my husband was targeted." She paused again. I gave her time. She sat in a quiet reflective moment. Only her lip moved as though she was about to speak. Then nothing.

"Why was he a target?" I prompted her.

"He was a target because he wouldn't go along."

"Go along with what?"

"I really don't want to say more than that."

"But Mrs. Parkin, we're kind of left here . . . what is—"

"All I know is my husband is dead and he was a good man."

"You say he's a good person, and yet you say he wouldn't go along with something. And this something got him killed?"

"I'm sorry. That's all I can say."

I stayed quiet, giving her time to reconsider. Then: "We're here because you called us. If you want to clear up your husband's name, fine, we're here to listen. But if you hold things back, we can't understand."

She dipped her head, letting her hair fall down around her shoulders. When she lifted her head, the lines around her mouth pulled downward with an arching frown. "Just follow the project and you'll see I'm right. He was a victim, and I'm still waiting for justice."

"And your husband never mentioned the project specifically?"

"I overheard him talking on the phone. We never talked about it, but—"

"You say your husband was picked up by someone. Who did your husband meet that night?"

Silence. I was ready to repeat the question.

"I wish I knew." She waved at the camera, indicating she was done. Ike shut down the works and waited. I kept thinking I gave up a vacation and the ire of Cat Miller for an uncooperative widow. The scales weren't tipping my way. If Amelia Parkin was using me to put her husband in a positive light, it probably worked. The interview would air on the newscast. I stacked it up as a way to keep in contact with her, hoping for the moment she would reason all the way and let me know what really happened when her husband stepped to the curb and got into a car.

Ike broke down the tripod, wrapped up the wires on the microphone and stuffed it in a carry bag. My news story would consist of Amelia's interview and nothing else.

She held up her hand. "Before you go, I have something to give you." I waited until she returned with a manila envelope, packed thick with paper.

"And this is?" I asked. She handed me the envelope.

"The police have the originals. These are copies. What you have is Grant's courier stops for the past three months. Inside, there are names, places, pickup points, everything."

"Why not let the police—"

"No. I want you to have them. You see for yourself if there's anything wrong there. I'm not hiding anything. This is why I called you. I want you to find who killed my husband and prove he didn't steal any diamonds." She pointed to the documents. "Now you have a copy and so does that insurance investigator."

"Frank Tower?"

"Yes." Her jaw muscles tightened. The right hand again rubbed the left.

"But these are only the stops that we know about. I mean, there could be others that he didn't put down or record?"

"I don't think my husband would do that. I trust you Mr. Bowens. Please, do what you can."

Chapter 29

I rested the half-eaten slice of pizza back on the plate, then pushed the food away from me. I wiped my hands on a towel and dragged the brown envelope closer. Outside my apartment, I heard doors closing and tidbits of idle conversation. I wondered when Cat would get the message I left on her hotel room phone. I decided to call her cell later that evening.

The envelope was perhaps a half-inch thick. I pulled out the sheaf of papers, making sure to keep them in the right order. Each page had a date, a customer name, a tracking number, and lines for describing the merchandise to be delivered. The first five pages all listed one single word: documents. The addresses were familiar but the customer names were not. I slid a reporter pad next to the envelope, flipped open a page, wrote down the word destination, and underlined it twice.

Grant Parkin was precise in his invoices. Each page was handwritten, but easy to read. On the tenth page, I stopped. For the company I saw a familiar name, L.M. Cornerstone Enterprises, Ltd. The date was two months earlier. Parkin's widow mentioned the connection before, leading me to meet the man with the pinky ring.

Parkin made deliveries to businesses, a hotel room, and even a yacht. I envisioned him racking up hundreds of miles a day crisscrossing the southeastern United States. Midway through the pile, I stopped again. The business listed was a location I visited twice during the week. First with Morgan, and a second with Ike. The Diamond-Escape, Ltd. jewelry store conjured up thoughts of gems and diamonds under glass.

On the page, under the word description, I found the words DIAMOND DELIVERY. But just off to the side, low on the page, I saw something else. NOT DELIVERED was written on the sheet. I flipped through the stack. On the top of each page, the word PAID was stamped in large red letters. So, who paid for the delivery of items not dropped off? And was there a stronger connection to Diamond-Escape, Ltd?

I checked my watch. Almost nine. I remembered the hours listed on the door. On Fridays, the Diamond-Escape stayed open late, until 10 P.M. I grabbed my keys. Maybe I could still catch him for a few questions.

Outside, the temperatures had taken a dip. It was a cold night even for Florida. I knew what Chicago felt like in January.

By the time I reached the parking lot, a hard ripple went through my shoulders. Aches and pains, I reasoned, from my gunshot wound. The palm trees gave me a certain warmth. Ten feet from my Beemer I heard something off to my left. I stopped walking for a moment. Palm fronds slapped together in the cross wind. I searched the parking lot.

"Matt Bowens?" The voice came from behind me.

I turned. "And you are?"

"Don't worry, I'm just an insurance investigator. The name is Frank Tower."

Chapter 30

He was perhaps six-four, with a small scar above his right eye. His shirt was starched, he wore no tie, and he had black running shoes. He kept his demeanor calm, probably not wanting to move closer, opting instead to reach into his charcoal gray suit pocket for a card. "I don't usually confront people in their parking lot. I prefer to work behind the scenes, but I didn't think you'd mind if I tried to see you." He extended the card. I took it.

"How did you find me?"

"Just like you, I have my ways about locating people." No smile. No emotion. Just a flat expression on his face.

"I was just heading out," I told him.

"I hope you don't mind, but it's not often I have any dealings with the press. I know this is awkward."

"Awkward? You say you don't like to confront people, but isn't that what this is?"

His jaw stayed rigid as a corpse. Hearing no response, I raised my key, ready to beep open the door of the Beemer.

"Wait a minute. Maybe we can both benefit. You know, share information."

"I don't share information." I pulled the key back.

"Okay, let's just say maybe you can help me confirm a few things." For the first time he took a step in my direction.

"You've got this all screwed up," I started. "We're not a wing of the police department, and we don't work with insurance investigators."

"I only want a second."

I said, "Mrs. Parkin said you were giving her a hard time."

"Just doing my job."

His posture was more anxious now. He flexed a fist of ebony fingers. "Amelia Parkin must have told you I work for the insurance firm responsible for the missing diamonds. I just thought I could work a few questions by you. And since I don't do that much through police agencies—"

"Frank Tower." My voice had the ring of confirmation. Reporters take in a collection of faces all day, logging them in their memory, focusing on their ties to others. And to news stories. After studying his face for the few minutes, I knew him. "Deerbay Police, right?"

"Former police."

For a moment, I thought I saw a flash of anger in his eyes.

"It's been what? Four years ago?"

"Not bad, Mr. Bowens. Four years and three months. That's when I left the force."

"Why didn't you stay?" I asked.

"Typical."

I heard the word, but his jaw barely moved. "Typical?"

"I came here looking for a little help, and I'm the one getting hit with all the questions. Now let me ask one."

"I can't—"

"Just hold it a minute. I want to talk to your friend. Cole Walker," he said.

"I saw him for maybe a second."

"Everyone seems to be looking for him." Tower's eyes kept a steady pierce. No blinking.

"You think Cole had something to do with the diamonds?" I asked.

He moved his arms behind his back and opened his stance as if someone told him to stand at ease. "I don't think anything. But it's my task to find the property, or find out what happened to it."

I said, "Who was paying Parkin to deliver the diamonds?"

"Can't help you."

"This is getting us nowhere." I let the car keys dangle in my hand.

"Okay." He said. "I'll give you something. Let's just say I'll give you this on spec. If you're able to give me something back, we're even."

"I can't do that—"

"Think about it." He paused, waiting for me to drive off. "That's all, my man, just think about it."

"Go ahead."

"Before you write off the warehouse and move on, why is it there were a number of meetings there, say, two months before your friend was shot?"

"Meaning?"

"Just check it out."

I took in his words. "Were they going to fire you from the force?" His body straightened up again. The fists came back to the front.

"That's what the newspapers said."

"Did they ever recover the money?"

"I passed two lie-detector tests." He paused. "One drug bust, the money turns up missing, and they automatically point to me. Now, I ask you, what is that about?"

"That was a lot of money," I said.

"Money is money, my man. I don't sweat over it."

"Seven hundred thousand dollars?"

Tower glanced at the ground, then back up at me. "They'll find it one day. Not from me, but they'll get it."

"Is that why you don't deal with police agencies?"

"It's best for me to do things my own way."

I held up his card. "Agreed."

Chapter 31

I waited until the next morning to see Dobb at the jewelry store. The Saturday morning crispness would last just another few hours until the sun churned up the temperature. The windows in the Beemer were down.

When I reached the jeweler, the place had just opened. Another shop owner unlocked a door and swept the walkway. Ike met me there. I cleared his overtime with Mike Brendon. Ike handed me the microphone.

One customer stood on the far side of the jewelry shop staring at a row of rings. A woman stood behind the counter but I didn't recognizer her. Dobb emerged from a back room, wiping his face with his hands, then squinting at me. "The diamonds I saw that night, still nothing on them, right?" he asked.

I shook my head. "We need to talk. I'd like to do this on camera." I walked him to a spot near the door. I waited for Ike to give me a nod, and I posed a question. "Grant Parkin was supposed to deliver some diamonds for you. Do you remember the drop-off?"

His face went ashen. "Mr. Parkin? I remember him. I

thought maybe you were bringing Morgan's diamonds back for a second look."

"I don't have them. But I have information about Grant. An invoice says he worked for you, that you hired him to deliver diamonds. Where were the diamonds going?"

"You don't understand." His eyebrows flattened over hooded eyes. "Nothing was delivered. Nothing."

"That's what the invoice says, no delivery. What happened? Was there going to be a drop? How was Grant involved?"

"Grant wasn't the point person, he was just a go-between." He paused again.

"Go-between in what?"

"You don't understand?"

"Were you ever in any meetings at the warehouse?"

"Maybe I . . ." He stepped back from the camera. "I don't want to say anymore."

"One man has been shot, another killed. How is Cole Walker involved in this?"

"You don't understand."

"Understand what?" I could hear my voice rising in volume to match his. "Fill in the pieces. What happened at the warehouse? Was Cornerstone Enterprises a part of all this?"

"I can't—" He ran to the back room. I turned to follow but the woman behind the counter blocked me and closed the door to the office.

"Get out!" She yelled. "Out now."

We left. Ike packed up his gear at the van, slowly rolling the long microphone cable, and packing the camera back in its case. "So what now?" Ike said, looking at his watch. "We're burning overtime, but if there's nothing to be done, I've got a long list of things to do at home."

"No problem."

Ike handed me the videotape. I tossed it on the front seat of the Beemer. "You can take off. The interview won't be used until Monday, but I've got to check on some things at the office."

I unlocked the door, turned off the alarm, and placed the videotape on my desk calendar. The air near the newsroom window was warm from the sun slanting in off the Intracoastal Waterway. I couldn't hear them but I saw bikini-clad bodies on boats, arms gesturing to the sky, and the constant flow of yachts cutting patterns of waves off gleaming white bows.

The stack of file tapes on Lopell's trials were next to a coffee mug. I grabbed the stack and headed for an edit bay. I looked at the tapes and the facts came down to this: Lopell received five years prison and two years probation in the first trial.

I checked the last tape of Lopell's last and final trial. I saw a familiar face. The face of a juror who held out for not guilty. The reporter on the story was Cranston, but the juror.

I stopped the tape and froze the video.

My jaw sagged in disbelief. On the TV monitor the lone juror was leaving the courtroom. His hand reached to wave at the camera. A hand with a large pinky ring.

Chapter 32

I got up early and put off going near Roland Campton of Cornerstone Enterprises until the next day. It was Sunday morning. I ate light, put on my sweats, laced up a beat-up pair of Nikes, and rolled the basketball out of the closet. On many Sundays Cat called and convinced me to dress for church in her old neighborhood. Cat was gone, and my routine was broken.

I parked the Beemer in the shade of a ficus tree. My stretching exercises over, I stepped onto the basketball court and took short shots first, feeling the basket, getting my range. My mind drifted to Cat, Shauna, and Jason. I had to make it up to them. They counted on me to come through, and I didn't.

The basketball court was deserted. I let the ball rotate in my hands, feeling the seams, lining up my shot, keeping my left arm straight, pushing off, watching the arc. All net.

The court time let me think. My mind was also sorting out the myriad of details surrounding the deaths of two people, a missing friend, and a briefcase full of diamonds.

I walked out to the top of the key and bounced the ball several times. I lined up the angles. On and off the court.

I thought about the connections between Campton and Lopell.

The ball spun momentarily in my hands.

I thought about Dobb the jeweler and Grant Parkin.

I bent my knees.

Morgan and the two large gems.

I jumped up.

Was Cole tied in to Lopell?

The apex of my jump. Hands set. I shot the ball.

Dead fingers protruding up through the mist in the everglades.

A high arc, in line with the basket.

Secret meetings in the warehouse.

The ball dropped into the basket. The net barely moved.

Cole's camera stashed in the garbage bin.

Half an hour later, I lowered myself into the contoured chair of my Beemer. I rolled the windows down, slid in a compact disc, let the voice of Luther Vandross fill up the car and leaned back. Now I felt the breeze.

I stayed in the shower twenty minutes before I toweled off. Dinner was of the microwave variety. By evening, I pushed a vase of flowers, long stemmed roses, into the passenger seat and pulled the seat belt across the sweat on the glass. The drive to Cat's was timed to hopefully beat them there. Once I arrived, I sat in front of her house and waited.

It was past ten when Cat's green van pulled into the driveway. I didn't know if she wanted me there or not. The lower half of the moon radiated against a gray-black sky. Once the van door opened, I helped with the suitcases. Jason was asleep in the back, but his body uncurled from the seat once the suitcases were moved. Shauna was the talker. "I went on the Screwball four times," she shouted. Her arms and hands made a looping motion. "It went like this until we were upside down."

"Yeah, it was fast." Jason was now awake, eager to tell me what happened.

"He didn't go on that ride," Shauna scolded him.

"I didn't say I did. I just said it was fast."

"What else did you do?" I put the suitcases near the front door. Cat pulled a set of keys from her purse.

"We rode the haunted mansion." Jason's face scrunched up, animated with the expression of a monster. "I didn't get scared."

"Yes, you did." Shauna bent over until her face was lined up with Jason's gape.

"No, I didn't."

"Yes, you did!"

Jason shoved Shauna. Two tiny hands pushing on the ten-year old's shoulders. She pushed back.

"Stop that, now!" Cat's voice echoed across the lawn. Shauna dragged her bookbag out of the van. The bag was noticeably heavier than before.

"What did you buy?" I asked.

"Oh, just stuff."

Cat had the door open and was inside turning on lights. She went through the house inspecting. Everything was in its proper place. Jason disappeared into his room. I heard the low thump of Shauna dumping the bookbag on the floor by the door.

"Take that to your room, Shauna." Cat looked tired.

Shauna's shoulders drooped. She picked up the bag and

entered her room. Cat turned in my direction. "So, Mr. Bowens, did you get that important story?"

"I'm still working on it, but yes, Friday was important. I'm sorry I couldn't make the trip."

"How's Cole?" Her expression was serious.

"We don't know."

"Don't know?" There was a raised arch to her eyebrows.

"He left the hospital. The doctors were still treating him and for some reason, he took off."

"Have you heard from him?"

"Nothing."

I left for a moment and came back with the roses. There was a glint in her eyes but no smile. She held the flowers in her hands and placed the vase on the coffee table. "Thanks, Matt. It's not your fault but I can figure on more missed trips?"

I couldn't answer. I wanted to pull her into a kiss but I just held my ground, waiting for a cue.

"Flowers don't always fix everything." Cat watched me for a moment, then stood with her head angled, a hand on her hip, and a mother's perception kicking in, probably listening for running bath water. "Excuse me for a second."

I dropped into the cushion of the couch and heard movement in the bathroom, the rush of water behind a closed door, muffled conversations between a mother and a son, the hard drop of shoes on the floor, and Shauna singing a song in a high-pitched voice.

Cat stood in the bathroom doorway, facing the tub. "You want me to stay and help you?" A pause. "No. You sure? Okay." She kept the door open. When she walked back, she readjusted the roses until the light caught them a certain way. "They are nice." A smile inched across her face.

"How was the trip?"

"It was great. I thought it was going to rain on us a few times, but it stayed dry. It was so crowded. We weren't the only ones to take advantage of a teacher work day." Cat bent her back, pushing her hands against her hips, stretching. "I'm beat."

"I'm sorry I couldn't make it." I stood up and softly dug my hands into her back and massaged tight muscles, rubbing in small circles.

"Oh, right there." Her voice was low and slow, almost a moan. "I hope it was worth it. These kids kept talking about what you were missing."

I kneaded my fingers against her back, stroking a downward, circular pattern, getting into her shoulder blade, caressing the ribs. Her eyes were closed. She leaned against me, until I felt her body's warmth. I kissed her once in the small area of her neck. Then again. My fingers were now working upward, starting at the slope of her back, and going inward until my fingers met at her spine. I kissed her again, this time on her right cheek.

Then I heard a voice. "Mommy, I need a towel," Jason yelled.

Cat broke off the embrace. She dipped once, turned, and I was holding air. Voices drifted from the bathroom. Take your time, I thought. Words first, embraces later. Cat escorted Jason down the hallway, his body wrapped in a towel printed with racing cars, water still dripping from his head.

I watched a single bubble float up through flower stems, rising in the vase until it disappeared at the surface. I sensed Cat's presence in the room, as if she was gauging me.

"If you're tired, I can call tomorrow," I said.

"Let's go outside."

We sat on the front step. The moon washed her face down in a sheen, a delicate brilliance in her eyes. I saw purpose there, an assurance and confidence I admired.

"We have to figure out more time for ourselves." I started. "You're making big decisions, and I'm left out. Even though I don't have a right to push you in any direction, we can still talk."

"If you mean the nursery, yes, I should have said something. I don't need you to sign off on what I do, but I like your advice."

She bent her head down, eyes at the ground, her hair tumbling around her shoulders much like the first night we met at a singles bar. I remembered my gaze had been so intense watching her, she locked eyes with my stare, then dipped her head as though embarrassed, letting the long strands fall and cover her face. When she looked up, her hazel eyes cut through the dark room. I put down my white Zinfandel, walked past talking couples, and introduced myself.

Now, I wanted to start over.

"We need to go to dinner this week. Somehow we have to squeeze it in."

She didn't respond. Then: "If you break this date, Matt Bowens," her words etched in defiance.

"Just give me a few days. I promise. Just you and me."

She leaned back, her face now covered in shadow.

"A promise? I've heard that before," she said.

"I'll be there."

"Okay." Her voice resounded with doubt.

"You're tired. I'll call tomorrow."

I pulled her toward me, letting the kiss linger. I got up.

"Goodnight," I said.

Chapter 33

"Great!" Ike said in disgust. He wiped his fingers, wet with coffee, against the side of his pants and looked down at the growing stain on the rug of the van. "Just another spilled coffee for the cause." Ike dragged his hand a few more times on his pants and gripped the steering wheel.

We sat in the parking lot in front of Cornerstone Enterprises. It was just after 8 A.M. Ike pushed the cup of cream-tinted coffee toward his lips.

"Why don't you let it cool down?" I asked.

"Can't wait." Ike said through a long sip.

Cornerstone Enterprises was the last in a series of corporate offices near Powerline Road. We waited for Roland Campton. Five minutes passed and his secretary arrived. She stepped out of a Lincoln Town Car. I heard the hard jingle of keys from our surveillance spot sixty feet away. She fumbled for a few seconds at the front door, then went inside. Lights flashed on inside the office.

Our goal was simple: Talk to Campton before he reached his office. Warned once about trespassing, we had no other option than to ask questions in the street. Others arrived to open offices. The building was a jumbled mix of noise and voices. I checked my watch. Eight-forty-five. This was the place I first noticed the yellow Porsche and its passengers.

An SUV rolled into the spot next to the Town Car.

"Let's go." I grabbed the microphone from the floor. Ike ran with the camera in his grip. When we approached the SUV, he shifted the camera to his shoulder. I pointed the microphone toward Campton before his foot hit the ground.

"Good morning, Matt Bowens, Channel 14. I see you did jury duty a few years ago. Now the former defendant is dead."

"And who is that? I didn't do jury duty." Campton flicked his eyes at the camera back toward me.

"Eric Lopell. We have you on video as a juror in his case. He was found dead."

Campton paused. Seconds passed as if he was weighing what to say. "Listen, I saw myself on television the last time you were here. It didn't look too good. You know, you and me pushing and shoving. I'm a businessman. I don't want any trouble."

"And your jury duty?"

"I remember it now. That was a long time ago."

"The defendant was Lopell. Didn't he do some work for you?"

Campton closed the door of the SUV and turned back to the microphone. "Yes, I was on his jury and yes, I heard his case."

"A hung jury."

"Correct. No verdict. But he never worked for me. I don't know where you're getting that stuff, but don't drag me into his death. I never really knew the man. All I know about him now is what you guys put on television and the newspapers."

He used his hands as he talked. The pinky ring flashed tints of gold in the sun.

"Lopell never went to meetings at your warehouse?"

"You keep getting on this warehouse thing. I told you, or rather, I tried to tell you, there is no connection to me. None." He walked into the building, and I watched the door close.

After ten minutes on a three-way phone conversation, Mike Brendon put down the receiver. The news director was on the other line, and I used the phone on my desk. I clicked off the line. Mike adjusted his glasses, pushing them up on his nose.

"Sorry, Matt," he said.

"I still think it's usable."

"The person who makes the last decision doesn't agree with you. And he's the boss, and his word is final."

I tapped the plastic rectangular box containing the interview with Roland Campton. I lost the second debate with the news director. The interview would not air on Channel 14, unless I had a strong, direct tie to the murder investigation. I needed a police announcement, anything placing Campton in line with Lopell.

"Just hold on to it." Brendon turned a sandwich around in his hands, as if looking for the perfect place to attack the mammoth hoagie.

"He held me back from mentioning Morgan's diamonds," I said.

"Think about it, Matt. We still don't know if those gems are somehow involved." Mike tore into the sandwich.

"There's just too much to ignore." Suddenly, Brendon stopped eating and picked up a piece of paper. "I got a call for you. They claim to be friends of Lopell. And they are angry." Brendon's words were slow and deliberate. "They didn't say come on over, but I know where they are eating lunch."

"Where?"

"The Perch Walk."

I heard Mike Brendon sucking the last swallow of water from a bottle; voices from the police scanners all garbled into one sheet of noise coming from the assignment desk.

"They say what they're angry about?"

"Not really. Miami called again." Brendon talked in between his chews. "Here's the deal. You get something major on this today or you're off to another story."

"There's more I could do—"

"That's it Matt. The producers have moved on. I know Cole is out there somewhere, but Miami is ready to let the story rest. We've got a major city council meeting coming up tonight with some hot-button issues. We could do an advancer."

"But I've got the rest of the day?"

Brendon paused. "Yes. The rest of the day is yours to look into this. But if there's breaking news, I'm pulling you off this." He took another bite off his sandwich.

I picked up my reporter pad. "Let me check this out. If you need us, call us."

Chapter 34

The Perch Walk was surrounded by dozens of palm trees. Paddle fans swept the air above a bar made of bamboo and mahogany. Weathered wooden slats covered the floor. A picture in the corner of the room showed a man ambling down a narrow walkway on the roof of a building. Under the frame, a large brass nameplate was inscribed with the words PERCH WALK.

Ike stood by the entrance, his camera resting on the ground. I saw a group of, perhaps, eight people jammed into one corner, glasses tinkling. A waitress walked by them, then stopped when one person in the group said something. She wrote down a couple of orders and left. I approached a man who had just tucked away a money stash in his pocket.

"I'm looking for friends of Eric Lopell." All talk ended. The faces had the same disdain. The money man was wearing a black tropical shirt covered in giant fish hooks. His hair matched his shirt. Down near the bottom of his khaki pants, he wore sandals and no socks.

"Why are you looking for them?" He had the expression of someone eager to be challenged.

"I'm Matt Bowens, Channel 14 and I—"

"A reporter." He was shouting now. His words carried above the room chatter. The group erupted in a smattering of laughter.

"The only thing Eric got from a reporter was bad news. Just really bad news." Money Man was hacking up something in his throat and he was looking around for a place to aim. He leaned over, glancing at my shoes. I braced for a flying lump of chaw. But if that happened, Ike would have to pull me off him and I would become the story.

He swallowed. "I don't see any of Eric's friends, do you?" The people around the table laughed again until the waitress arrived with a tray of beers.

"If Eric doesn't have any friends here, then I'll move on. I was looking for the person who called my station . . . someone to talk about his death. It just seems odd, he wasn't in any trouble and now he's gone."

Money Man turned. We were facing each other, eye to eye. "You've got some nerve coming in here." The smell of stale beer hissed through his teeth.

"I just want—"

"I know. You want trouble. Is that what you're looking for? I can give you a whole lot of trouble." The fingers in his right hand balled up.

The waitress put down the last beer. "Don't want no problems in here. Been through that." Defiant, she placed the tray flat against her skinny frame and crossed her arms.

"We called because everyone is getting the story wrong." Another voice. This came from the opposite end of the table. His voice was small, almost impossible to hear.

I said, "All we've heard is one side about Eric Lopell. Someone killed him and still there's no one to speak up for him. I'm told he was clean these last few years, and yet he's somehow mixed up in something and now this." I paused to see if money man was listening. "If no one wants to say anything, trust me, I'm out of here. I'll just go with the information I have."

Money Man grabbed the handle of a beer mug, aimed the thing at his mouth and sucked down the drink. Suds streaked the side of his face, running down into his stubble. From the other side of the table, Little Voice pushed his beer back next to his plate. He had a scar just over the sunglasses he wore, even though he was inside. When Little Voice pointed to the door, I noticed his right index finger was missing. "Let's do this outside," he said.

"I'm Adrian Moxer." Money Man had a name. Arms fixed alongside his body, he refused my offer to shake hands. I guessed he was about six-foot-three. Thin wisps of hair were all that was left on top but he had plenty on the sides, which was swept back to a thick ponytail. Ike positioned him so the sun lit up his face.

"So, you're ready to talk?" I asked.

"Someone has to speak up for Eric. And that's me."

I raised my microphone. "Was Eric Lopell in any trouble at the time of his death?"

"Eric was straight up clean. No problems. The man got a bad rap in the news. He did his time, got released, and I don't know who would take him out like that."

"Did he ever say anything about who might want to give him trouble?"

"Eric Lopell was an all right dude. I haven't seen him

in awhile, but he kept his life clean, he stayed away from trouble. This is a surprise to us."

"Surprise?"

"Sure. I mean, when he was in the business—"

"Stolen diamonds?"

"Yeah. Okay, he was into that. But that was a long time ago. Back then, he had tons of friends, 'cause he had money. Cash breeds so-called friends. And when you don't have it, they're gone. That group in there," He pointed to the restaurant. "They never left."

"When was the last time you saw him?"

Moxer drew a hand across the top of his head. "I don't know. Months maybe."

"So, what happened?"

"I don't know. I admit there is a blank part in his life I don't know about. But something did happen. Before that, he was clean."

"And in the last few months?"

He paused. "I came out here to say good things about him. We had some good times. But I just got worried that someone got his attention in the wrong direction. He never called for help. At least not from me. I would have kicked him in the right direction."

"Any thoughts on who influenced him?"

"I wish I knew. I just wanted to say he wasn't as bad as you guys make him out to be."

Ike lowered his camera, aiming the lens at the ground. Moxer pushed both hands down into the pockets of his jeans. "If you hear of anything, let me know."

I took down his cell phone number and I gave him a business card. He was almost to the restaurant door, then stopped and turned. "We're doing our own investigation. We're looking for the guy who killed him."

The door opened. I heard the easy harmony of a love song riding the cool January air until the door closed shut. I gave the microphone to Ike. When I looked up, I saw her standing in the parking lot. The half moon rings below her eyes were now larger. The hair was bunched up in back, strands pointed in all directions. Before I spoke, she held up her hand to stop me. We stood, mannequin-like, waiting for her to speak.

Morgan Walker stepped closer until the sun caught her in a bad angle, pooling her cheeks in shadow. The cracked lines in her lips moved. "Follow me."

Chapter 35

Morgan's car moved faster than the rest of the traffic.

"Don't lose her." I checked her passenger seat. She was alone. "So, where are you taking us?" I spoke under my breath. Her car cut in front of an SUV, causing the driver to slam on brakes. Ike waited until he had a moment, then stomped on the gas pedal. Our van chugged past the SUV and the snarling face of its driver. We turned right on Third Avenue, past shops and small restaurants.

"I don't know if I can keep up." Ike shouted. Morgan veered right again, after traveling halfway through the intersection. "I thought she was going straight." Ike's fingers pulled hard on the wheel. Tires squealed as he turned. Ike shook his head, his jaw muscles tight with frustration. Twenty seconds later we made another right turn. A woman was about to cross the street, then stopped when Morgan drove past her. The woman shook her fist as we swept by. Morgan's car pulled away from us, moving faster.

"She's gonna kill us." Ike said. He leaned forward, straining the seat belt against his chest. Morgan finally slowed down for the first time. She pulled in behind a county bus. The Perch Walk was on my left.

"We're going in circles. She's trying to see if we're being followed." I watched her put a cell phone to her ear. The conversation was quick. We reached Third Avenue again but this time she turned left. We motored up an entrance ramp, joined interstate traffic, got off four miles later, and headed north into a suburb of Fort Lauderdale.

A narrow canal bordered the avenue. This was an older section of the county, untouched so far by developers. Morgan turned onto a dirt road. The property was huge. A line of trees gave way to thick bushes of wild periwinkle. After three more turns, a house was tucked away on my right. The place was a single story job, toylike in appearance next to a ficus tree. The air was cooler here, tempered by the layers of tree limbs shutting out the sun.

Morgan was in the house before I could say anything to her. The door was left open. Ike unpacked his gear. "Ready?"

We entered a room with cathedral ceilings and striped wallpaper. The crumpled bag of a fast-food chain was the only thing on the kitchen counter. Ike carried in his gear, snapped the camera into the tripod slot and waited.

Cole Walker stepped into the middle of the room.

He favored his right shoulder, walked stiff and held his hand out like he was holding on to an imaginary cane. He gripped the arm of the couch and eased himself down into the cushioned leather swells. He let out a soft grunt as he dropped down. Tendrils of pain lashed across his face. Cole breathed through his mouth.

"Hello, Matt." He looked at Ike's gear. "It's a bit weird being on this side of the camera."

"You know what I always say? I'm just looking for the truth." I tossed my pad on a coffee table. "How are you feeling?"

"Like a man who's been shot." He tried to smile, but his lips reverted back to a tight line. His eyes stayed fixed on me, as if to pick at my core, rip down pretenses, and scour inner thoughts.

I compared him to the last time I saw Cole Walker. The determined eyes were the same, but his weight was down. A sliver of gray hair arched from front to back above his left ear.

"How did you find me?" I looked around for Morgan, but she was nowhere in sight.

Cole shifted his right shoulder a bit inside the shirt. "I called Mike Brendon. He told me. But I made him promise not to warn you or no interview."

"You know the drill better than I do. There's a lot I want to ask you—"

"Okay." He cut me off. "I'll do this but don't beat me up if there are some things I can't get into."

I didn't answer him. He leaned back into the puffy folds. I got a chair and placed it near him. Ike nodded from behind the camera. I raised the microphone and posed a question. "Did you kill Grant Parkin?"

Cole blinked. He tilted his head down for only a moment. When he lifted his eyes to me, I saw a spark of anger. "No soft buildup questions for you." A half crack of a smile dented the even contour of his jaw.

"The question is still out there. Did you kill Grant Parkin?"

"No."

"He was found murdered in your car. What can you tell us about that?"

"I have no idea how he got there. The first time I heard about that came from Morgan. I never saw him that night. I left my car at the warehouse." He paused. "I can honestly tell you I had nothing to do with his death. Nothing."

"Who shot you?"

Cole sat silent. Moments passed.

"Who shot you, Cole?"

"I can't get into that."

"Did you see the person? Did you get a good look at a face?"

"I can tell you I was being beaten. Fists. Kicks. I didn't think I was going to live. And then there was a shot."

"Who was doing the beating?"

"Not yet. I'm just not going to answer that right now." Cole paused. Then: "All I can tell you is I went to the warehouse to meet a client. But when I got there, I was jumped. It was dark and there were two of them—maybe they were after my equipment. I fought back but when you're up against two men and a gun . . ." Cole winced. "After the shot, I just don't remember anything except waking up at the hospital."

"Why were you meeting a client at the warehouse?"

"I can't say right now."

"The people who hurt you are still out there. Are you going to the police?"

"We're calling them, yes."

"And your injuries?"

"The bullet passed through my right shoulder. I'm lucky because there's very little internal damage. I'm told

I'll have full movement. The bruises will heal. But I'm extremely lucky. A few inches over . . ."

"Why not stay in the hospital?"

"I'm getting my treatment. I'm in good care. I'll be fine."

"Cole, who are you running from?"

"Running?"

"Yes. Weren't you supposed to stay hospitalized? Who are you hiding from?"

"One reason I agreed to sit down with you and talk to Channel 14 is because I've known you for a long time. And I want everyone to know I'm still here. I'm alive. I'll get better and better. If anyone thinks I'm on the run, I want them to know I'm not going anywhere."

"Grant Parkin was carrying diamonds. You have any idea where they are now?"

"I keep telling you, I never saw the man. I don't know anything about his diamonds."

"Parkin's wife said someone picked him up at his home. You, perhaps?"

"It wasn't me."

"What about Roland Campton of Cornerstone Enterprises? You have any dealings with him?"

"I don't want to keep saying this, but certain areas will remain off-limits for now."

Cole pressed his left hand into the area where he was shot. "It's time for a new dressing."

"The warehouse where they found you, did you ever attend meetings there? Meetings with Campton?"

"Look, Matt. I'll answer a few more questions about me and my health, but that's it. I'm not going to get into some kind of speculation about me or the last few months. I just won't."

"Morgan showed me some rather large diamonds. Where did they come from?"

"The diamonds are mine. Free and clear. And they shouldn't be part of any investigation."

"What's the connection, Cole? You worked for Cornerstone, your jeweler is tied to him, Grant Parkin did work as a courier for both of them. Where do you fit in?"

Cole let out a laugh. "You and your assumptions. It's guilt by association. Let it go, Matt, there's nothing there. We all did some small jobs. Nothing special."

"What kind of small job?"

"A freelance job. I'm a stringer, remember? I shoot video. You know that. That's how I make a living."

"You can't say what the job was?"

"My client is owed a bit of privacy."

"The police will be asking. Did they ever question you about Grant Parkin or your shooting?"

"They are next on my list. Trust me, I'll be contacting them."

"So detectives never had a chance to speak to you?"

"Not really."

"The day I spotted you and Morgan at the warehouse, why were you there? You forget something, like your camera?"

"That's it Matt. Interview over."

"I want to know. What brought you back to the place where you were shot?"

Cole squeezed the alligator-style metal clip, releasing the lavaliere microphone from his shirt. He dropped it on the sofa and pressed his left arm into the cushion to get up. I kept firing questions.

"Why did you come back to pick up your camera?"

Silence.

"What's so important on the video?"

Nothing from Cole.

"What kind of meetings were going on in the ware-house? What did you do that made someone shoot you?"

The lack of a comment from Cole only made me talk louder. "Two men have been following me. One of them is now dead. Does the name Eric Lopell mean anything?"

Cole stopped. For a moment, I thought he might hook up the microphone again. Instead he headed for the door.

"You worked on his trial. I thought maybe you got to know him after the court case." I was speaking to an open door.

Ike unsnapped the camera and followed Cole. I picked up my pad. Cole was in the front yard now, a mottled pattern of sun spots and shadow creeped across his back as he walked. Just yards off, Morgan was waiting in the car. Two suitcases were in the back seat.

Cole turned back to me. "You can stay as long as you like. The house is yours. We'll be somewhere in Florida, but we won't be be coming back to this place."

"Turning your back on a murder case?"

Morgan opened the car door a few inches, then slammed it so hard the car shook. Cole stood there glaring at me. "You think I want to be doing this?"

"Cole, get in the car." Morgan was animated. Her head kept twisting as if to keep Cole in her sights.

"The very people I relied on, the people who were supposed to be looking out for me, almost got me killed."

"Cole!" Morgan was screaming at him.

I stepped closer. "What people, Cole? Who?"

Ike pushed the camera to his shoulder. I aimed the microphone at Cole. "Tell me."

"Cole, we had this all worked out. Get in the car." The lines tightened in her face and pulled against Morgan's jaw.

"We can straighten this out, Cole, if you want." I kept my voice even, trying to calm him.

"You have a piece of information about The Maker." Cole was a few feet away from the dark imprint of the ficus tree and a slant of sunshine caught him in the forehead. "I'll leave you with this—"

"Cole, shut up! Now!" Morgan quick-stepped toward him, her arms waving wildly at the air. She tried to get in Cole's face.

"Who is The Maker? Grant's wife wasn't sure." I yelled.

A smile burned across the width of his face. "The Maker—" Cole began. The smile turned into a burst of laughter.

"Cole stop, please." Morgan was next to him, almost pleading. She stood between Cole and the camera. He moved to side-step her block, but his mobility was off. He raised his left arm to keep her off. "Your info is wrong."

"What's wrong? Who is The Maker?" I asked.

His shoulders sagged, and he let Morgan gather him in. She was in the midst of pushing his wounded body into the front seat of the car. Then I heard him yelling at me. "The Maker isn't a person."

Cole settled in his seat. Morgan stomped around the side of the car, got in, and drove off. The back tires spun, churning up the turf, spitting pebbles at our feet. The car disappeared in a billowing cloud of road dust. Ike kept shooting video. A gust out of the northeast chopped the top off Morgan's cloud. I lost her behind a collection of Brazilian pepper trees.

Chapter 36

"Now that is incredible." Mike Brendon reveled at the picture on the television monitor. His eyes were two bulging blue pools through his thick lenses. Brendon was at the controls of the roof camera, pushing the small joystick forward so the picture moved with his command. He stroked his beard then put his hands back on the controls. "This is great."

I looked over his shoulder. "Can that thing zoom in?"

"Oh yeah, watch." He pressed a button and the picture pushed into a closer view of a yacht. The boat was all fluid motion cutting across the top of the water, pushing waves to the side. "I've got 50X and 100x and beyond. I can't read the newspaper on board the yacht, but I can get a good look."

I guessed three or four phone lines rang at the same time. Brendon stepped away from the control panel. "I love that thing," he mumbled at the machine.

Yards away I heard Ike queuing up sound clips from the Cole Walker interview before editing them into a news story.

"So, you got a lead story?" Mike Brendon was back behind his console of police scanners, telephone phone bank and stacks of newspapers, faxes, and press releases. "I looked at that interview three times. It just doesn't sound like Cole. I mean, he sidestepped a lot of questions."

Ike said, "A man was found dead in his car. Maybe he's got something to hide?"

"Police have never mentioned him as a suspect," I started. "If Cole's DNA isn't on Grant Parkin, and if they swabbed his hands for gunshot residue and came up flat, then maybe they ruled him out?"

"Maybe." Brendon's voice carried over the sound of the scanners.

"And The Maker . . ." I said to the open side of the room.

"Any thoughts on that?" Brendon turned down two radios.

"All this time I thought it was a person. Since it's not, I've got to rethink this. The Maker could be a store."

"Good luck." Brendon turned to his pile of papers and ringing telephones. I sat at my desk and tapped the computer keys until I was on the internet. I typed in the phrase, The Maker, and waited. A search engine gave me more than fifteen million sites, all connected in some way to the phrase. I clicked on dozens of sites. There was nothing connected to diamonds. Ike finished editing the story and we fed it by a direct phone link to Miami. Once there, they played the story as the lead at 6 P.M. After the taped segment, I gave a live in-studio wrap-up.

By the time I reached G.G.'s nursery, the sun was a memory and the night sky was lined with ink-tinged clouds. I scanned the grounds looking for Cat. Ground mist seeped into a row of potted palms grouped along the back edge of the property. The air was layered with gardenia scent and stacked packages of fresh mulch. I saw her eyes first. Her gaze cut through the Everglades imprint of black trees. When I reached Cat, I took her hand. Fingertips first, then a clasp. There was a certain roughness as I touched her fingers. They were working hands now, coated with dirt. I didn't mind.

"What are you doing way out here?" I asked.

"Just sorting through my mind what needs to be moved up front." We were wrapped in night sounds. The chatter from birds and pigfrogs drifted on the breeze.

"I had a good day." She pulled her hand from my grasp and rubbed the earth from her fingers. "Sold a bunch of plants." She searched the nursery as if taking an accounting of what was taken by customers.

"Glad to hear it." I turned in the direction of the front gate. Cat matched my steps. "I want you to know . . . ," I started, "I'll do better in the future. I've got to carve out more time and don't let things get in the way of our relationship."

Cat didn't respond. I picked up a small rock and tossed the stone into the darkness. "It's not worth it to get you upset."

"If you're going to do some conceding, I've got to do the same," she said. We stopped at the steps of the cashier's hut. Cat reached to push her fingers through her hair, then stopped and looked at her hands. "I've got to wash up."

"Ya'll spending too much time in the dark back there." G.G. Everson smiled and turned off a computer. "Did Cat tell you we had a very profitable day?"

"She told me."

G.G. picked up a set of keys on the table. "Yeah, a good day. I love it. It's just January, but people want to get a jump on spring planting." She lowered her voice. "You can do that in Florida, ya know." G.G.'s laughter smothered the cascade of animal grunts still coming out of the glades. "And there was that one guy." G.G.'s eyes widened.

"I sold him ten plants," Cat said.

"I tried to get his attention but he went directly to you," G.G. added. "Good look'n' black man," G.G. shouted. Her words rolled out slow and enthusiastic as the smile on her face.

"So, where are the kids?" I asked.

"My neighbor is watching them. Their daughter is in Shauna's class."

I helped G.G. push a long gate into position. Then she snapped a lock into place and tugged on it. "Goodnight." G.G. got into a pickup truck, heavily dusted with road grit. She waved once and drove west toward the protected lands of West Broward County. G.G. was among a small group of homeowners who lived at the edge of civilization and the Everglades.

"I'm glad you sold so many plants."

"I'm really enjoying this." She placed her hand on her hips. My car was parked next to her Honda. "You going to follow me home?"

"No phone calls. I promise." I let her watch me turn the thing off.

"Good."

"So, who was this man who bought nine plants?"

Cat said, "I stopped him at ten plants. Was it ten? I

don't know, maybe more. He just seemed to pick plants at random, almost like he was in a hurry. And he had a heck of a time getting them into his car."

"Maybe he should have used something bigger," I said.

"Maybe. But his car was nice. I mean real nice."

"Really?"

"Yeah. I hated to put the plants inside, so I put down some plastic. I didn't want to get anything dirty. The interior was perfect." Cat paused as if thinking about the car. "He was driving this bright yellow Porsche."

Chapter 37

Cat didn't wait for me to respond. She was behind the wheel and down the road before I formed a question to her about the man in the Porsche. I started the car and followed Cat. If this was the same man, why was he tracking Cat? I figured the target was me. I checked my rearview mirror for a Porsche close on my taillights. Nothing. With every stop and each lane change I kept checking the street for the sports car.

Inside ten minutes we were in Cat's driveway. I waited for her to let Shauna and Jason out of the car. Once inside the house, both scampered to their rooms.

"They've already been fed." Cat said, glancing at her watch. "I've got some great leftovers. You hungry?"

"What did he look like?"

"What did who look like?"

"The man at the nursery. The guy driving the Porsche?"

Cat's lips bent into a smile. "Matt Bowens, a man of jealousy." Her eyes sparkled as bright as the smile.

"I'm not jealous. It's just—"

I turned from her, stepped off the distance to the front

window, and glanced into the purple shadows. In the glass I saw Cat's face reflect an anxious look.

"This is getting spooky. Why are you checking the window?"

I left the window and moved close enough so Jason and Shauna wouldn't hear me. "I think the man in the Porsche has been following me. And now, I'm pretty sure he's found you."

I saw question marks in her stare. Her eyebrows angled inward. "Why? I don't understand this. The man seemed so nice."

"Did he give you a name?"

"I never asked him."

"Did he ask your name?"

Cat paused. "Yes, I think I did. But that doesn't mean anything. He was just a man buying plants. He paid cash and left. That's it."

"Give me a description."

"Matt, this is nuts. You're getting paranoid over a customer you've never seen? And that's not jealousy?"

The door to Shauna's room opened. A face edged past the side of the door, her fingers gripping the frame. "I heard arguing."

"No one is arguing. Now back to your room." Cat's voice was still at the high volume level.

"No arguing, please." Shauna leaned against the door.

"We're not arguing. Now go. We're talking. That's all. Talking. Go."

The tiny face moved back inside the room. Cat whispered: "She's used to me and my ex shouting at each other. I know we kept her up all night sometimes."

"C'mon Cat. I wouldn't be saying this if I didn't

think something could be wrong. What did this guy look like?"

Cat breathed a long sigh. "He was about your height. Maybe a bit taller. His skin color was about the same as yours."

"What about hair? Short afro?"

"Really short. He had a nice smile, and he was very courteous."

"And he paid in cash?"

"I told you that already, yes."

"What about a name?"

"I didn't ask."

"No name?"

"Are you hearing me okay? I said he didn't give his name."

"What about Cole? Did he mention Cole Walker even in some remote way?"

A veil of frustration creeped into her eyes. "He just bought plants."

"Cat, I was out doing an interview and this yellow Porsche pulls up. Two people inside. I think he is one of them. The other guy is dead."

"Dead? When?"

"The day before you went on your trip. Shot to death. It's one reason I couldn't come on the trip."

"Who was he?"

"A diamond thief from years back. Supposedly he was retired. They found his body out in the Glades."

"And what? You think this guy in the Porsche did it?"

"I don't know. I'm worried about you."

"I'll be fine."

"Fine? G.G.'s Nursery isn't that far from where they found him."

Cat bunched up her shoulders and extended her arms in the air for emphasis. "You don't know anything about this guy. Nothing. So why judge him like that?"

"It's not that way. For one, he's driving a stolen car which belongs to a dead man. And he might be tied in to all kinds of things. Does G.G. have a gun?"

"Gun?" Cat was shouting. The doors to the rooms of both Shauna and Jason opened. Two sets of curious eyes bore into me.

"We're not arguing." Cat gave each word its own time and place. "Now, back inside." The doors closed.

"Well, promise me this," I started. "If this guy comes back, call the police, then call me."

"And if I call the police, what am I going to tell them? This rather nice guy who was kind enough to buy ten plants from me is a thug who needs to be arrested?"

"Okay, if you want, forget the police. If he comes back, call me. Immediately."

I let the silence build as a buffer. Cat slumped into a chair and crossed her legs. Her right foot tapped the air with a quick pace. Another twenty seconds passed before I spoke. "You've got to trust me on this. We've been in a bad streak between us. But this is one time when you've got to hear my side. If that guy comes back again, call me. I want to be there."

Chapter 38

Detective Victor took almost four minutes getting to the telephone. After a voice told me to hold on, I pulled out my pad and waited.

"Victor here."

"Good morning. Bowens, Channel 14. Did Cole Walker ever talk to you?"

"If he did, I can't discuss what he told me."

"But did he contact you?"

"The homicide office is in contact with Mr. Walker, yes." Then Detective Victor fell back into police speak.

"And did he give you a statement?" I asked.

"Not yet. But we know where he is; if we need him, he's cooperating. And yes, we will speak to him soon."

"Is he a suspect in the murder of Grant Parkin?"

"Not at this time."

"Has he been ruled out?"

"No one has been ruled out."

"So, there are no suspects right now?"

"No."

"Have you determined Eric Loppell's connection to all of this, I mean, since he was a diamond thief?"

"We're looking into that. I will tell you that it's clear to us that he wasn't killed at the scene."

"Is there an active search warrant for any location?"

There was a long pause. Victor was probably figuring how to answer without telling me too much. "You would have to check with the records department."

"So, there is an active warrant?"

"I'm not saying that. Just check records."

"Did you find anything to help you at Lopell's home?"

"We're still sorting it out."

"Let me go back to the search warrant." I was stalling. In many cases, detectives liked to keep it quiet until their work was done and then they filed the paperwork. "There's a good chance the clerk's office won't know about it until later."

I waited. Victor still wouldn't give up the info. I moved on. "What's the connection with diamonds?"

"I wish I knew. There's a thread there, running through all of this, but we haven't linked it yet."

"Lopell died from from a gunshot. Just one shot?"

"I can't get into specifics, but we announced at the scene he was shot." He paused. "I hate to run but I have to go."

We ended our conversation, and I put down the receiver.

"Hello, Matt." The voice coming from the other side of the room was familiar. I turned. Bill Cranston was the same height and weight, but everything else was different. What was left of his hair was now gray. Both cheeks and his nose were splotchy. "The doctor burned off the pre-

cancer molds," he said. "The sun down here can getcha if
you let it."

"Have you ever been to this studio?" My hand pointed
to the bank of lights and the logo.

"Naw, first time. We used to be up on the twenty-
seventh floor of the old Steggers building. Not this."

Cranston was a Broward County television reporter for
twenty-seven years. He retired and taught high school
kids about broadcasting.

"So, you covered the Lopell trial?" I sank back in the
chair.

"That's why I'm here. Mike Brendon called me in. Said
you might need some background help."

In the corner, behind the noise coming from police
scanners, Brendon waved.

"I might need some help. What can you tell me about
Eric Lopell?"

"Lopell was a weird one. Very particular. He always entered the courthouse the same way, through the back.
Even though it was longer, he didn't care. That's just the
way he was."

"Did he ever do an interview?"

"A sit-down? Never. Just the old throw a microphone in
his face and get a two-word answer. That's about it."

Cranston pulled a chair from a desk and placed it in the
middle of the room, far from the sun rays. He shied away
from the slants of warmth coming through the window
with the apprehension of a vampire. "Can't sit in the sun.
Doctor's orders."

"Did you ever notice Lopell and Cole Walker . . . how
can I put this, working together?"

"Working together? You mean planning something?" Cranston shifted in his chair. He worked a piece of gum in his right jaw. His muscles flinched and relaxed with the chews. I let him settle the question in his mind. Finally: "Yes, now that I think about it, there were a few moments."

"Like?"

"Well, during one of the trials, the second one, I think, we split up for lunch. I came back early and found Eric talking to Cole. It didn't seem like small talk either. They got quiet as I approached."

"You ask him about it?"

"Sure. In my own way of course. I didn't want to accuse him of anything but it just seemed odd. He just said they were talking about sports. I let it go."

"But Cole always worked the trials?"

"He was the main photog on all of them. Cole didn't want any other photographer to work the story. It was his." Cranston stopped chewing. "You know I just thought of something. About six months ago, Cole called me. He was all excited about some project."

"Did you get involved?"

"I had to turn it down, too busy at the school. But the offer sounded fantastic. I just couldn't do it."

His jaw was in motion again, working at a faster clip.

"What kind of offer?"

"He wanted me to do some voice-over work. It's been a long time since someone paid me to use my voice for anything other than teaching."

"But what made this offer stand out?"

"Well, I kept asking him what the script or idea was about, and he stayed kind of coy about the whole thing."

"And?"

"And, when I kept pressing him, he said it had to do with diamonds."

"Diamonds?"

"Yes. He was shooting some in-house video about gems and he needed me to voice the track to go with his video."

"Did you ever see a script?"

"No. When I said I couldn't do it, he never called back."

"Did he describe anything about the video or the script?"

"Just a bit. I like to know all I can about a product before I put my voice on it. Even though I'm not on the air anymore, I've got a reputation. He told me . . ." Cranston let his gaze drift to the ceiling then back at me. "He warned me not to say anything about this."

"You're not under any kind of contract obligation. What he told you is free information."

"He would really be upset with me if I told you—"

"Look, someone shot Cole. He's a beating victim, and he's on the run. The man didn't even stay in the hospital to get well. He took off. If there's anything out there to catch the thug who did this, then yes, I'm asking you to tell me what was Cole working on?"

"Okay." Cranston said. "I just feel bad because I don't think the project got off the ground. But . . ."

"Just get it out in the open. Then we'll deal with it."

"He said the project was called The Maker. It had to do with some new device. In fact, I think the device was called The Maker. That's all he told me because I wasn't supposed to hear all that. Not unless I was going to do the script."

"And you said no?"

"No to the script, no to the whole thing. It just didn't seem right."

"What did Cole say?"

"He was upset. Real upset. He was counting on me to get involved and when I didn't, well, that kind of set him off. The next thing I heard was a loud click in my ear."

"Did he mention who else was involved in project?"

"No, it didn't get that far." Cranston pushed a hand over the thin arrangement of white hair. "I hope I don't get Cole in any trouble."

"Trouble found him a long time ago."

"Matt, I think I've got to send you out." Brendon was shouting over the voices on the police scanners.

"What's up?" I said.

"I just caught a word or two on the scanner and then they went to a another channel, one that I can't hear. But I got a location. It's your friend, Mr. Pinky Ring."

"Cornerstone Enterprises?"

Brendon was back into a silent mode and nodded. His eyes were directed at the bank of scanners, ready to pick up a comment or location. He resembled a man in a trance. Ike walked past me, holding two camera batteries. Cranston stayed in the office, as if absorbed by the trappings of the job he left behind.

A uniform waved us past a row of unmarked cars and we parked near the driveway of an office building. The front door of Cornerstone Enterprises was propped open. People either stood outside talking in low tones or carried boxes. Each person was stonefaced, wearing a navy blue jacket with F.B.I. on the back. Three others with hand trucks pushed boxes out to a waiting van. Ike was out and shooting video before I flipped open my reporter pad. When the F.B.I. conducted the search, I expected no statements, or interviews. I fell back on the one thing I was given: observation.

I spotted Pinky Ring's secretary standing next to an agent. Her hair was a stack of wayward curls as if she just woke up. The agent just stood listening to her talk at a rapid pace. I checked each unmarked car, looking for him in a back seat, but Campton was nowhere around. Three local uniforms stood off to the side, I guessed as a courtesy since the search was in their jurisdiction. I pulled my cell phone and called O'Donnell. He answered on the third ring.

"Morning."

"It's Bowens. Officially, what are you working at Cornerstone Enterprises?"

"Officially? Nothing. I can tell you that we're giving back-up assistance to the F.B.I. on a federal search warrant."

"Are they taking over the Cole Walker case?"

"Nope. That's still ours."

"Then what are they doing out here?"

"You'll have to ask them."

In my mind, I saw O'Donnell smiling, knowing he could hide behind an investigative search warrant and tell me squat. Over my shoulder, an agent almost dropped a load of boxes. Not one expression changed. Each person had the persona of someone on a mission, professional and serious. I thought back to what Detective Victor hinted about a warrant. It didn't have to be him serving the search order. I sensed O'Donnell's impatience through the phone.

"Any update on Eric Lopell's death?" I asked.

"We got some calls and we're following up on a few leads, but nothing to say at this time."

"How are Lopell, Parkin, and Walker tied into the F.B.I. search?"

"You're on your own with that one. Let's face it, someone stepped on a few big toes. And they crossed over the state line to do it."

"Federal probes just don't start overnight. How did this kick off? Phone conversations? Federal wire tap?"

"Happy hunting Bowens." My cell phone flashed the words . . . call ended. Ike was busy getting video of the unloading of boxes from all different angles. Low ground shots with his camera an inch off the grass, to walk-back shots with Ike backpedalling, stepping the same pace as the agent. I held off calling the F.B.I. spokesperson for a few minutes. I recognized the face standing next to the news van. I approached.

"What are you doing here?" I said.

"Just following the trail." Frank Tower was wearing a Florida Marlins baseball cap, worn jeans, a loose fitting cotton white fishing shirt, and a pair of midnight black sunglasses.

"I see you caught up to Mr. Walker. I saw the interview on TV."

"And?"

"Thanks to you I got some idea of what happened. But I'd still like to talk to him."

"He's running from someone."

"He can't run that far. Like I said, I'm just following the trail."

"The trail just got cloudier," I said.

"Confused? Step into my office." The insurance investigator pointed in the direction of a Ford Explorer. Once inside, I let the rush of air-conditioned breezes sweep across me. Tower leaned back across the console and pulled a thin briefcase from the back seat. He plugged a cord into the lighter and popped open the case. The wide screen of a computer lit up the inside of the SUV. "I take my work with me."

"And what are we looking for?"

Tower typed in several letters and he was on the Internet. A wireless connection was probably handy in his line of work. He pushed the computer to my side of the car.

"Go ahead. Type in the name of, what do you call him, Mr. Pinky Ring?"

"Yeah, Campton."

"I've got you on a national database. Go ahead."

I typed the name inside the search block and waited. Within seconds, I saw Campton's name and two addresses.

"You don't have access to something like this, but I do." Tower's sunglasses dropped down a bit and he pushed them back into position. "But believe me, the information here is accurate."

The cursor flashed in front of a home address and a business location. I recognized the last entry as the address for Cornerstone Enterprises.

"Okay," Tower took the computer back from me, typed in a new Web site and pushed the laptop back in my direction. "Now, check his criminal background." I looked down. Next to Campton I found blank spaces. Nothing.

"So, he's clean. I knew that because we checked days ago."

"Alright." Tower's voice had a certain lean to it, etched

in sarcasm. "Let me have the computer again." The large screen gave me a side view of what he was doing.

"You don't have access to this either. I do because I'm working for a company, and authorized as a—"

"I get the picture. You've got the inside track. I don't. What's the site?"

"I punch in Campton's social security number. And—"

"How did you get that?"

"Later on that. For now, let's just concentrate on this. Now, check this out."

I looked down. The screen was flashing INQUIRY in bold red letters.

"What does that mean?"

"How much do you know about Campton?"

"Just that he's a big property owner. There's the warehouse, and the office here. A string of people worked for him, including Cole and Grant Parkin."

Tower looked out at the swarm of F.B.I. agents taking control of the grounds. "I don't know what's in those boxes, but I have an idea they won't find everything they're looking for. This man is too good."

"What are they supposed to find?"

"I'm going to make this clear for you and then back out of the way and let you do some of the grunt work."

He paused. Tower took his right hand and adjusted the baseball cap a tad lower on his head. His face was as tight and serious as the people hauling out boxes of paperwork. He pulled his hands back, interlocking his fingers, his voice was even as the horizon.

"It's very clear. The man you call Pinky Ring." Tower paused. "There probably is a Roland Campton, all right. Somewhere. But the guy you say is Campton doesn't exist."

Chapter 39

"**I**dentity theft is tough." Tower took off his sunglasses and tapped them against the driver's side window. "All it takes is for some fool like Campton to go Dumpster diving, go through your garbage, collect your social security number, name, address, phone number, and become you." He lowered the window and talked to the air. "They take your name and the stink can stay with you for years."

"He's been here a long time. He even worked as a juror on a case."

"And?" Tower pushed the sunglasses back over the brown eyes glaring at me and raised the window. Nervous energy. He had a cop's attention to details around him. His eyes never stayed fixed for long, glancing left to right, yet always taking in each of my words.

I hoped Tower was ready to fill in some blanks. Tower's words hit the dashboard. His eyes were aimed at the F.B.I. agents. "He probably took a name from someone living in another part of the country. Someone who died, or just grabbed a name. People can get married, get a driver's license, empty bank accounts, have a family, buy homes, and take on a new life just by claiming to be someone else."

The F.B.I. agents ended their march of boxes. A person who appeared in charge closed the front door and pressed a strip of red crime tape over the knob, sealing the office. I opened the door to Tower's SUV. Before I left I had a question: "Why are you helping me?"

"Because down the road a bit, I need a favor."

Tower's SUV rolled to the other side of the street and stopped. Sandra Capers and her photographer pulled up just as the unmarked cars were lining up to leave. Her photog moved fast, pulling out his camera and recording video of anything that moved. I motioned to the person I thought was in charge of the warrant crew. I got within twenty feet of him when he yelled some unintelligible words about contacting the information office in Miami and kept moving.

Frank Tower's SUV was gone long before the F.B.I. vans pulled out into traffic. Campton's secretary was in the back of an unmarked car in the caravan rolling out of the parking lot. I called Brendon.

"The F.B.I. say anything?" I asked.

"Officially, here's what you can use. They say this is an ongoing investigation into possible violations of the RICO act and they can't name a target just yet," Brendon said.

"Racketeering, eh. That means they've got people on audio or on tape conspiring to do something. Cole must be caught up in it."

"They won't comment off the record, but I've got my thoughts."

"Like?"

"Mr. Pinky Ring hires Parkin to do some work and it backfires."

"He doesn't exist."

"What?"

"I had someone run down a check for me. The guy stole someone's identity. We've got to track him down all over again. Call your contact at the Social Security Office. See if they'll confirm there's a separate investigation into Campton. And I need some file tapes."

"Which stories?

"All the stories I did on Grant Parkin, the interview with Cole, and the first story on the warehouse."

"You got it."

Twenty minutes later the live truck pulled into the parking lot of Cornerstone Enterprises just as my cell phone chimed.

"Matt?" Brendon sounded out of breath.

"I'm here. You okay?"

"Fine . . . had to run a videotape to a crew waiting outside. I got some information for you."

I let Brendon pause. "So, what's the deal?"

"You're right. The man we came to know as Campton is set to be arrested for identity theft. The paperwork isn't finished yet. These are state charges."

"Okay. What else?" I set my pen to paper.

"You can say there's an open investigation into I.D. theft going back some five years."

"That's it?"

"For now. They say in about two days, it should be wrapped up and they can arrest him."

"How does this tie into the F.B.I.?"

"That's not clear yet."

"Thanks."

"Mike gave me these." Hank, the live truck operator, handed me a stack of three videotapes.

"Thanks." I fingered the stack, pulled out one in particular and slid the tape into the play deck. A large number ten was frozen on the monitor until I hit the button. The numbers rolled down, nine, eight, seven, until I heard my voice over video of Campton's office.

"What are you looking for?" Ike propped his camera in a corner of the truck.

"Just a hunch." My eyes were on the monitor. I watched the story two times, checking the video, looking for anything. I watched Campton's expression, the hand coming up in my face, the confrontation in the office.

"Wait." I hit the pause button. "You see that right there."

Ike stared at the small television screen. "I don't see anything."

"There," I pointed. I placed my finger on what looked like a metal plate on a desk. "You see that?"

Ike leaned into the monitor until his face was just inches from the glass. "What?"

"That!" I put my index finger directly on the spot. "The nameplate on the desk. It says Janice Lacey. That's the secretary talking to the F.B.I." I reached for my cell phone.

"Channel 14 . . ."

"Mike, I need a minute of your time."

"What's up?"

"Run the name Janice Lacey. I don't have an address,

and her car wasn't here to check on tags. The feds gave her a ride, but she's Campton's secretary. I need everything. Home address, phone, any arrests, the works."

"Not before noon, I hope?"

I checked my watch. Eleven-fourteen. "No. Not for noon. I'd have to double check it anyway, but if we get something, I'd like to run on an address this afternoon."

Chapter 40

I finished my live report for the noon and watched Hank roll in the long cables of wires when my cell phone rang.

"Hello."

"Is this Mr. Bowens?" The voice was feeble. I strained to hear her.

"Yes. It's Bowens."

"I hope you don't mind. Your office gave me your cell phone number."

"It's okay. Who is this?"

"You probably don't remember me. I met you when you were trying to see Mr. Campton. I'm his next door neighbor."

"I remember. How can I help you?"

"Well, I promised if I saw him I would give you a call."

I pushed the phone into my ear. "And?"

"Well, Mr. Bowens, he's here right now. Or I should say he's outside, driving around."

"Driving around?"

"Yes. He keeps circling the block. I don't understand

why he doesn't just park in his spot. I mean, it's his house and his spot. What is he waiting for?"

"What kind of car is he driving?"

"I don't know. It's red. Nothing fancy. Just red. I saw you on television. Is Mr. Campton supposed to be in jail?"

"No. That might change in the near future, but for now, he's free to come and go. When was the last time you saw him?"

"Just a few minutes ago. He stopped across the street, just sitting there in his car. It's really strange."

"Thanks, we're on our way."

I ended the call. Ike was already in the van waiting for me.

"Let's head for Pinky Ring's home."

"What's there?" A look of uncertainty in his face.

"If we're lucky, Campton. He's been spotted circling the block."

Three blocks later, Ike zoomed through a yellow light, a few notches above the posted speed limit.

"Going around the block?" Ike whispered.

"Obviously, he's looking for the feds. He figures the place is being watched, so he's taking his time, really checking things out."

"So, he must really need to get in the house?"

"Sure. By now, he knows his office has been swept. His secretary is talking to the F.B.I. He has to get something out of that house before another search warrant comes down."

I called Brendon. "Listen, we're headed to Campton's house. He may still be there if we hurry."

"Fine. Just stay in touch."

Ike slowed the van two blocks from the row of houses

in the subdivision. He went another block and stopped. We watched the lot, and I scanned the area. No car. No sign of Campton. I eased the van closer. Then I saw it. The red Chevrolet was parked between the houses, backed in, with the trunk door up. Pinky Ring was moving stuff. I shoved the gear into park and pointed to the car. We were out and walking. Ike followed my direction, staying out of the view of the front windows. We approached from front sidewalks and lawns next to the car. I took the microphone from Ike.

The front door opened. Campton stepped into the sun, apparently confident no one was watching him. He was taking a bag of garbage to the street. We waited. When he turned around, Ike's camera was recording.

"Mr. Campton, Matt Bowens, Channel 14. Why was the F.B.I. searching your office this morning?" His eyes widened as if to take in the entire picture. He stood there for a moment, shock flashing across his face for only a moment.

"I have nothing to say to you."

"They took out boxes of evidence. We're told it's part of a racketeering probe."

He kept his gaze away from me and didn't run. His pinky ring stayed at his side, instead of shoving a fist into the camera lens. He appeared to be thinking how to answer.

"I have nothing to hide. They won't find anything."

"If that's the case, why was the F.B.I. there?"

"I'm not exactly sure yet."

"What is The Maker project?"

A muscle in his cheek flinched. His eyes blinked. I watched his mouth form a word, but nothing came out. Finally he said, "What are you talking about?"

"Cole was involved in it, others know about it. The Maker."

He stood quiet for a moment. "I want to be clear about this. Whatever Cole got himself into, it's not my concern. I don't know anything about . . . what did you call it, The Maker? What is that?"

"Cole was a key part of the project and there's a connection to Grant Parkin," I said.

"The man found shot to death in Cole's car? That's going a long way trying to associate me with some bogus plan from Cole Walker. And then a murder? Forget it. I don't know anything about it."

"I'm told it worked out of your warehouse?"

"People rent from me. I don't know what they're doing in there. It's not my business."

"And who do they make the checks out to? What's your real name?"

Before the sentence was finished, Campton was on the move, pushing past my microphone, making a direct line for his car. I kept pace with him. Ike, camera and all, started running.

"We understand Campton is not your real name. You're under investigation for identify theft." His pace quickened. Ike kept up with me. We matched his jog. "How did you get the name?"

Nothing.

"How long have you been using the name Campton?"

He kept running faster.

"Why was Eric Lopell coming to see you that day?"

"Who?"

"You know him, Eric Lopell. You were a juror on his

trial. Lopell, the diamond thief. He was coming to see you. Why?"

"I didn't have any association with a Mr. Lopell."

"Did Eric Lopell know the real deal?"

He had reached his car by now. He slammed the trunk and got behind the wheel. By now the camera was bouncing off Ike's shoulder with each lunge. The window was down and I pushed the microphone toward Campton. The engine fired up and the car lurched past us. He shouted at us as the car rolled over a line of red impatiens. "I didn't kill Lopell!" And then he was gone.

Chapter 41

"Good job." Mike Brendon nodded with the smile of an assignment editor with an edge on the other channels. Scoring an interview with someone under federal investigation will do that. Ike sat on a bench just outside the back door, chewing a turkey sandwich.

I logged the videotape, taking down notes on comments made by Campton and marking the corresponding numbers on the counter. Later, during editing, I'd refer to the numbers for Ike to put the video package together.

What intrigued me was what was in the trunk of Campton's car. When he pulled out, I wrote down the tag numbers. Brendon ran the tag and it came out to a different address than the home, office, or warehouse. A check of the map showed the address was eight miles west of Fort Lauderdale. If he had another house, that would explain how he disappeared from one location and never returned for days until a neighbor saw him hiding in the street. He probably stayed away from his warehouse, the office was closed by the F.B.I., and he had to enter his house like a thief. Campton was a moving target.

Brendon stood over me, a wry smile connected both cheeks. "Miami has you in two shows. You're the lead at five, and the second story at six. And they want some tease video of the interview you got."

"Then I guess I better get busy." I rewound the videotape until I had a picture of the very first few seconds. The image filled the large monitor. Campton carried a large garbage bag to the corner. I reasoned he wouldn't leave anything in there to implicate himself. The bag had the round shape of things shredded. I fast forwarded the tape until I had an angle of his car. The trunk was not visible.

"Hey Mike," I yelled. A few seconds later, he strolled into the edit booth.

"What?" He sounded impatient, as if he might miss something while being away from the scanner for twenty seconds.

"The woman who called. You got her number?"

"Sure. I'll put it on your desk."

I pulled the tape from the deck and returned to my desk to call the neighbor. The phone rang several times before she answered.

"Good afternoon. This is Matt Bowens. Thanks for the lead on Campton."

"Thank you. I don't like him very much. I saw you outside."

"That's why I'm calling. You have a window overlooking his side door?"

"Yes. He parked that car of his over there, and he nearly smashed my roses."

"Could you see what he was putting in his trunk?"

"Yes . . . ah . . ." I pictured her thinking, eyes drifting

over the nicknacks in her room, recalling the scene in her mind of what Campton was stuffing in his trunk.

"Well, he had some paperwork," she started. "And a computer. He put a computer in his trunk."

"Anything else you can remember?"

"Yes. It seemed he was carrying some of those video things."

"A camera?"

"No. It was more like what you store the tapes."

"Videotape boxes?"

"Yes. He had a bunch of those. Just threw them in the trunk."

"Thank you."

Chapter 42

My report ran almost four minutes. Long for television. I stood in front of Ike's camera and showed south Florida the interview with Campton, denying any involvement, the identity theft probe, and the F.B.I. investigation with the seizure of records from Cornerstone Enterprises. I withheld saying anything about The Maker until I had more information.

As soon as I removed my microphone, I thought about Cat. Her plant-buying customer could return. One comfort was knowing Cat and G.G. together, two strong women, would pose a problem for any thug. I sat down prepared to call the nursery before I left. That's when the phone calls started. The first one came about three minutes after my report aired. Two more came within seconds of the first. Six more after that. Then ten more.

Brendon sent me the first caller.

"Can I help you?" I said.

"Why are you guys mess'n' with Campton?" His voice was firm.

"I'm not messing with him," I told him. "He's a target in a federal investigation."

A short pause on the phone. Then: "Thanks to him, my portfolio is doing just great. I'm up twenty-two percent because of his program."

"Program?"

Another pause. "We've kept this a close secret up to now." His tone was less anger and more reflective, as if he was gauging his words.

"Maybe I shouldn't be telling you all this," he said.

"Just help me out. Give me a hint about this program."

"I'm just an investor. That's all. If they arrest Campton, it's going to cost me a lot of money. They need to back off."

"Look, I don't understand. Is it okay if we do an interview?"

"Go on television? No way."

"Then make it clear for me. If I may ask, how much money did you invest?"

"Almost thirty-eight thousand dollars."

"Thirty-eight thousand? And you were buying into what?" I asked.

"That's what we were supposed to keep quiet about. You won't hear about this on the Internet, on TV, or in the newspaper. It was all word of mouth."

"Again, for your thirty-eight thousand dollars, you were investing in what?"

"Let's just say I was was doing just fine. My dividend checks were pretty good. The money was rolling in."

"And the product?"

I heard the even peal of dial tone.

Mike Brendon held up his hand, showing four fingers,

meaning there were four phone calls waiting for me. The phone rang. He changed his hand to indicate five. I picked up the line.

"Matt Bowens . . ."

"Yes. Why are they doing this to such a nice man?" Her voice had a slight draw on the letter *a* in each word, like someone from the Midwest.

"He's under investigation."

"Well, they ought to let him alone."

"Are you an investor?"

"Yes. I've been a part of the program for more than a year now."

"And if I may ask, how much did you invest?"

"One hundred-twenty thousand dollars."

The numbers were starting to roll in my head. Staggering numbers of money, and I only talked to a couple of people.

"What were you investing in?" I asked.

"We were given details of the project, and I must say, the results were incredible. But we were instructed not to say anything or we could lose our investment."

"And let me guess. They didn't want you to talk about it, but they you were encouraged to tell others to invest?"

"Why yes. I got my father involved and my sister in Illinois."

"Did they put in a lot of money?"

"All together, probably close to two-hundred sixty thousand."

"Can we do an interview with you?"

"Oh, no, I can't do that. They wouldn't want me to do that."

I said, "We're looking for someone to defend Mr.

Campton. If you feel strong about how he treated you, then why not say what you're telling me on the phone?"

"I'll have to think about it."

"And you feel safe about your investment? I mean, can you sell back your stake and get your money back?"

"Why would I want to do that? So far, the investment is doing just what they said it would do. I just want the government, the police, and you reporters to leave Mr. Campton alone."

I heard dial tone again.

Brendon was pleading with me to pick up another line. But I asked him a question first. "Are any of these people willing to leave a name and a phone number?"

"No one."

"Okay," I said. "Send the next one."

"Are you the reporter who did the story?" The voice was energetic but quiet.

"Yes. Go ahead."

"I'm calling you from work, so I can't talk too loud. I hope they put Campton in jail for life."

"What happened?"

"I had second thoughts about the whole deal. I mean it just sounded too good. I don't know about anyone else, but I haven't received anything recently. No dividends, nothing."

"Did you complain?"

"Oh, sure. I called every day but got nowhere. I threatened to go to the police, and he kept promising me I would get my money in the coming week."

"And did it come?"

"No. Not a cent."

"How much was your investment?"

"I was a founder. So, the amount was substantial."

"Founder?"

"As far as I can tell, I was one of the original members of the investment club. My portion to join was just over five hundred thousand dollars."

"And at first, the returns were good?"

"Yes. At first. Then things got slower and I called more, but I kept getting put off."

"Are you willing to talk about this on camera?"

"I have no problem with that. Maybe it's the only way I can get my money back."

"Sir, if I can, what was the project you invested in?"

"I'll tell you that when I see you."

I took down his name and address. Ike had already agreed to work late. I decided to call Cat from my cell phone.

Chapter 43

A guard let us into the parking lot. Then he buzzed a side door and we were let into the lobby of an upscale condominium. We thanked the guard, and Ike pushed the button in the elevator for the sixth floor. When we got off the elevator, a door was open down the hallway and a gesture from a man in a gray sport coat led us into his condo.

The walls were brushed paint on concrete. No wall board. All the pipes were exposed.

"The architect wanted an urban rustic look." He held out his hand. "Logan Murray," he said.

I introduced myself and Ike. We both let our gazes drift around the large expanse of the room. A floor to ceiling black and white photograph of the Everglades took up a huge section of one wall. Ike set up the camera near the couch. I pulled up a chair.

"I've never been interviewed before."

"How long have you lived here?"

"In this place, just eleven months. But I've lived in south Florida for close to thirty years."

Ike nodded. The camera was recording.

"Why did you invest so much money?" I asked.

"I was promised returns of at least twenty percent. And in this economy, when you hear promises like that, you listen."

"And did those promised returns come in?

"Oh yes. The first six or seven months, I was smiling."

"And with your five hundred thousand dollars, you were buying into a part of what?"

He took in a long breath. I imagined him thinking it over one last time. If he talked to me, he risked violating the terms of his investment agreement.

"I'll tell you," he started. "It's just that there was a clause in the paperwork stating we forfeited our money if we talked about the nature of the investment."

"Is that legal?"

"Maybe. Maybe not. But it was still a signed contract between myself and Campton."

"And . . ."

"I'll probably never see my money again, so what am I violating?"

He rubbed his hands together and for a moment looked down at the concrete floor.

"It's up to you," I said. "But you could be warning others not to get involved."

"I was buying into a company selling high quality diamonds."

"Did you see any of these diamonds?"

"Yes. Every investor is given a chance to look over the goods before making any final decision."

"And you were convinced?"

"Yes. I had all kinds of people telling me not to invest and I couldn't really discuss it with them because of the clause."

"And yet they wanted you to recruit other investors?"

"Oh yes, that was made very clear. They just wanted me to steer other people to the deal, and they would do the rest."

"Did you do that?" I asked.

"For a while. I feel bad about that. It's one of the reasons I'm talking to you. I got at least four people involved. I was going to propose the idea to a few more people. But . . ."

"You had reservations?"

"Yes. At first, when the money kept coming in, I didn't question anything. But I did some digging on my own."

"And what did you find?"

"As far as I could tell from my questions, each investor had money. Plenty of money before this deal."

"You didn't need to invest?"

"I'm a very wealthy man, Mr. Bowens. It would be very embarrassing for any of us to admit we got ripped off when we were supposed to be such smart business people."

He looked at a nearby coffee table as if a drink was supposed to be sitting there. "We weren't expected to complain," he said.

"But you did complain?"

"Yes. Several times. I complained about the late dividends, where was my money, how I could get it back. I got no answers. I just feel—" He stopped. I let him work through the ordeal of telling everything to a camera and eventually an audience of television viewers. "I just feel bad. I convinced some close friends to put up their money for this."

"Who introduced you to the deal?"

"I don't know. Somehow Campton found me. I guess I was ripe. But when he showed me that DVD—"

"DVD?"

"Yes. When you spend that kind of money, you're supposed to get something. The DVD came a few days after my conversation with Campton." He started to get up.

"You're still wearing a microphone," I warned him.

"Sorry. I was going to get a drink." Murray sat back down.

"We're almost finished," I told him. "Do you still have your DVD?"

"Sure. It's very good quality."

"And so were the diamonds?"

"Yes. That's what got me hooked in the first place. If you know anything about diamonds these were among the finest I've ever seen."

"Did you buy any of them?"

"We were told investors couldn't purchase them, no."

"Didn't that send up an immediate red flag? You couldn't buy the very thing you invested in?"

"It should have but it didn't. Greed does that."

"And what part of the world were the diamonds coming from? South Africa?"

"You mean a mine?"

"Yes. It takes a lot of work to get them out of the ground."

Logan Murray smiled for the first time. "That's the beauty of these diamonds," he said. "They didn't come from the normal source. These diamonds were supposed to be machine made."

Chapter 44

We watched Murray turn on his DVD player and the ninety-inch wide high-definition television on the far wall. He hit the play button and as the video played, we heard classical music over scenes of diamonds rolling in slow motion on a soft surface.

"Look at them." Murray's face and eyes were mesmerized by the gems. A smile lined his face. "You see why I invested."

The stones were impressive, especially on a large television screen. What I suspected was confirmed when I heard the narrator. The voice spoke of crafting gems so perfect, they would surpass earth diamonds in color and sparkle.

The voice belonged to Cole Walker.

Ike looked at me. "You can tell his photography work. I recognize those slow zooms."

In Cole's narration, he said The Maker could produce dazzling diamonds. And The Maker would make the investor rich beyond dreams. In the twelve-minute presentation, Cole showed a machine purported to be able to produce big volume, show-stopper quality diamonds, using a device to duplicate the high pressure and heat needed to make a diamond. In the end, the results, according to Cole, were spectacular.

Indeed, the gems were impressive. They glowed and threw slants of color around the room. We never saw Cole, only heard his voice, along with hundreds of angles or facets of the production gems.

"Can we have this video for a few days? I'll give it back to you."

"No problem," Murray said.

"Have you been contacted by the F.B.I.?" I asked.

"No, but after this interview is shown, I'm sure I'll get a call."

"Why didn't you come forward before?"

He paused. "Because when Campton first appeared on television, we all got a reminder not to say anything, that it was an aggressive reporter with a nothing story. Well, that nothing is turning into the arrest of Campton. That's when I decided to pick up the phone."

"Thank you."

We left. Down in the lobby, the guard let us back into the garage.

"So Cole is in this thick," Ike slammed the camera case hard, as if Cole betrayed every journalist and photographer.

"I don't know Cole's direct part in this. We just know that's his work on the tape. Remember the carpenter who saw someone carrying in light cases. That had to be Cole down at the warehouse, producing the tapes for Campton."

"So was Cole in on the scam?" Ike asked.

"We don't know that yet. Maybe he didn't know. He could have been duped into making the tape."

"And maybe not." Ike closed the car door with the same hard slam.

I held open my pad and wrote down a reminder to my-self to check on Campton's secretary in the morning. "If these ripped off investors found out where to find Lopell or Cole, the list of suspects could really increase."

I was playing the sides again, sizing up angles, and comparing bits of information until I had a good picture of how the scam worked. "I bet copies of these videos are what Campton's neighbor saw him packing in the trunk."

Ike peeled out of the parking lot. "He's cleaning up be-fore the feds find it all."

Chapter 45

My day didn't end until 11:15 P.M. I put together a news story that included the new interview and information. It wasn't until ten minutes before the 11 P.M. newscast that I got the phone call from police confirming the diamond scam. The federal probe centered on phone calls and deals made across state lines to induce people to buy into The Maker.

The deal worked like many others. You convinced a small group of so-called investors to part with their money. And at first, you gave them some of their own money back, telling them it was their dividend or a return on their investment. The unknowing victims told others to get involved. Word spread and, in time, there would be a network of victims all sending in cash. All Campton had to do was sit back and collect. But all scams get that stink on them at some point. Once Campton pocketed the money, victims were given excuses instead of cash. Get-rich quick gimmicks like this one were as old as the days of selling swamp land.

In short time, the feds would corral Campton. My immediate concerns were multiple. I needed to find Cole Walker again. Did Campton kill Grant and Lopell and shoot Cole?

I counted twenty-seven messages left on my desk by Mike Brendon. All of them potential victims taken in by the lure of making diamonds only to find their money had turned to coal.

When I got home, a message from Cat was left on my phone. Her voice sounded reserved, almost as if our relationship was going in two different directions. She wanted my input on a big decision, and I wasn't there. I failed to make a planned trip. And when I was supposed to be enjoying dinner with her and the kids, I left early. I looked at the phone and decided it was too late to call her. Our talk would have to wait.

"Man, I need some coffee." Ike Cashing rubbed his eyes and stretched his body through a yawn. "This is getting to be a tough schedule. Up late, and back into work early."

Playing out a hunch, we sat outside the Greenpark Apartments, hoping to catch Campton's secretary. Her big-sized car was twenty feet to our left. I glanced at my watch and noted it was 7:15 A.M.

"Maybe she's not going to work," Ike said.

"From what I understand, even though the F.B.I. left in the afternoon, police didn't release the building to Campton for hours after that. This will be her first time to go through and find out what they took."

"And then probably call Campton."

"I doubt if he cares," I said. "I'll bet Campton is busy getting another identity."

Before we settled into our parking space, we circled the lot twice looking for Campton's car. It wasn't there. At exactly 7:30 Janice Lacey walked down from her second-floor apartment to her car. I didn't consider her a suspect, so I didn't treat like one. I approached without Ike. No camera. Instead he stayed off to one side, his camera on the ground.

"Excuse me, I'm—"

"I know who you are," she snapped.

"I'm just asking you, off-camera, if you wanted to do an interview about Cornerstone Enterprises. I mean, did you invest like others?"

She gave my question some thought before answering. "I was told not to say anything."

"By Campton?"

"Well, yes."

"Did you know that's not his real name?"

"Why . . ." She mouthed the next few words but nothing came out. Her mind must have been a swirl of comparing inside information with the facts out in the open. "He never said anything like that to me. Who told you that?"

"Again, did you invest in The Maker? That's what I want to talk to you about. A lot of people did and they can't seem to be able to get their money back. What you say could help."

"What I say could get me in trouble. I don't know about this." She looked down at her car keys and inched closer to the door.

"If what you saw looked clean, then that's fine. There's no one to speak for Campton."

"Just one question." Her voice was so low, just barely audible amid the squawk of car horns traveling the nearby boulevard. Ike reached down and pulled the camera to his shoulder. I took the microphone.

"Your thoughts on Campton?" I asked.

"If there was anything wrong, I didn't see anything." Lacey shifted her weight from one foot to the other. A movement of nervousness. "Mr. Campton always treated them nice, and I never thought anyone was not getting the service they paid for or a return. I mean, everything was going along just fine, until the police arrived."

"No one ever called to say there were problems?"

"Not really. I mean, I got a couple of calls with people complaining, but I always just gave them to Mr. Campton. He took care of all that."

There were so many questions I wanted to ask, but the wrong one would trigger her to shut down. Still, I had to push it.

"Why would Eric Lopell be coming to see Campton?"

"I have no idea. I just worry about my own problems."

She clicked on her car keys and the door unlocked. She reached for the handle. "Besides," she said. "I haven't been paid in almost four weeks. I'm quitting."

"There was a man riding with Lopell. Did you know him?"

The car door opened and she got inside. I had less than ten seconds to get an answer. "Who was he?"

"Leave him out of this."

The car door almost took the top off the microphone. Janice Lacey backed up and never glanced again in our direction.

Mike Brendon stood over my shoulder as I typed on the keyboard after going over notes from the interview with

Janice Lacey. I kept working out in my mind how I could find the man who was riding with Eric Lopell.

"There's really only one place where I can search for him," I said. "And that's the street."

Chapter 46

Channel 14 arranged the next two hours of my life. Mike Brendon set up a meeting with seven victims of the rip-off scam at their lawyer's office. They were eager to talk, probably buoyed by the notion of firing off a lawsuit before Campton was arrested. Ike brought in six video-tapes, and we sat down and recorded each grieving tale. One was a retired judge, another owned a string of tire stores, two had just sold companies up north and moved down, and the last two were tied to old money. All of them bristled at the thought of why they didn't see a pending problem. Each chronicled large amounts of losses. The size of the scam was huge. Just seven victims alone to-taled more than a million dollars.

They told me how Campton lured them in, telling how they were on the ground floor of a new invention, and they were set to reap thousands of dollars a week from the na-tional sales. Only the judge was visibly upset about the loss since it affected him the most out of the group. I had enough tape for a half hour special. The one down side is no one knew any faces other than Campton. No Lopell, Grant Parkin, or any nicknames surfaced out of the long interviews.

And they spoke of seeing diamonds. Not just on video-tape, but real diamonds. The victims say they weren't allowed to take or buy any, just hold them to see the end product of what the machine could do.

"My fingers are about to drop off." Ike relaxed the grip on the camera and flexed his fingers.

Interviews over, Ike packed up his gear close to 11:30 A.M. Before we drove into a fast food spot, I decided to make a stop a few miles east of the lawyer's office.

I stood before the front door of the Diamond-Escape, Ltd. and tucked the folder under my arm.

"You think he'll talk?" Ike opened the rear door of the van and sat on the bumper.

"I can try."

Ike followed me to the front door. Sankerman Dobb, the jeweler, opened the door for us. His eyes had the look of someone who stayed up through a long night.

"Gentlemen," he said. His voice sounded tired.

"I wanted to ask you about the deliveries by Grant Parkin."

"The police have already been here." He took up a position behind the counter. "But I don't mind telling you some of what I told detectives." His glance broke away from me and toward the trays of gems. "You ever heard of an attorney firing the client? I think that's what's going to happen, because I won't follow her advice to shut up."

Ike shouldered the camera, but Dobb shook his head.

"I'll tell you the information, but that's it. Not on-camera just yet. In time, but not today. You still want to listen, or just leave?"

Ike put the camera on the ground. "I'm here to listen," I said. I pulled out my folder and opened it to the sheets of invoices given to me from Amelia Parkin. "Recognize these?"

Dobb examined them with the curiosity of someone going over a tax audit. "I do," he said.

"If Grant Parkin made deliveries for you, how come some of these say 'not delivered'?"

"It was probably his code."

"Code?"

Dobb picked up the papers and spread them across the glass counter. His index finger landed on the words 'not delivered.' "He made those deliveries then they came back to me."

"Let me guess, Campton needed some flash."

"I guess."

"You guess?"

In the world of drug dealing, undercover police used so-called flash money to entice and show the seller they had the goods.

"Grant Parkin delivered for me, but I had no idea he was using my diamonds as part of a rip-off. And I'm ready to say that on camera."

Ike set up the gear and for the next few minutes Dobb told me he never suspected anything until he got a call from the federal authorities.

"I never saw this man, Roland Campton," Dobb said. "I only dealt with Grant Parkin."

I explained the dealings of the scam. "It's into the millions," I told him.

He shook his head.

"And Parkin never said anything?" I asked.

"No, not a word. I stayed in this until we had a problem."

"You mean the shooting of Grant Parkin."

"He was a good man, I don't care how this investigation ends. But I lost a shipment of diamonds that night."

"Did you tell the police?"

"Not at first. I just told the insurance company there was a robbery."

"And they sent Frank Tower?"

"Yes. I was afraid the police might say I was part of the rip-off. But I'm not."

"How much are the diamonds worth?"

"Just over four hundred thousand dollars. Maybe more."

"Why wouldn't they just buy the diamonds and use them all the time?"

"I guess these guys were smart enough that they didn't want to be tied to something that tangible. Besides, one of their savvy investors might notice the same diamond coming at them months later when it should have been sold."

I gathered up the sheets off the counter and slid them back into the folder. Ike went ahead of me. I stood in the doorway ready to leave. Dobb held on to his counter like a man looking for stability.

"Just one more thing," I said. "Would your missing diamonds be enough for you to kill Grant Parkin?"

"The one thing I can tell you for certain is I didn't kill anyone."

I reached Ike's van as my cell phone went off. It was Mike Brendon.

"Are you headed this way?" He said.

"Why?"

"You've got a visitor."

When we reached the office, Amelia Parkin was waiting for us.

"Did the paperwork help you?" There was an anxious look on her face. Her question hit me before I got all the way inside the room.

"You didn't have to come down here. All you had to do is call." I set the food on my desk. Ike disappeared into an edit booth.

"I'm sorry, I should have called first. I was downtown and I thought I'd come by." Her usual waist long hair was tied into a ponytail.

I said, "Your information was very valuable. I was able to trace some stops made by your husband." I paused, going over the information in my mind.

Parkin eyed a chair and sat down. "All I know is he did what he was told and they killed him."

"But you have no proof of that."

"I don't, but I'll continue until I find it. I thought you were going to help me." As she spoke, her fingers raked through the long tresses, pulling apart the ponytail until her hair shook with each word. "This chair is warm." Her voice was iced in anger. "That's because you are spending too much time sitting instead of investigating."

She was pointing a finger at me, shouting each word. "I gave that information to you. Just you."

Ike stepped back in the direction of his camera, but I

waved him off. "Let the police do their work," I told her. "They also have your list. And they'll put a face on this."

She lowered her hand. A stone calm came over her face. "They have found a killer." Her veins etched down her neck.

"What killer?" I asked her.

"You see! You have to get your information from me. It should be the other way around, Mr. Bowens."

"What are you talking about?"

"Did you see what police found in Eric Lopell's home?" Her voice remained kicked up in volume.

My answer was slow in coming. Too slow for Parkin. "I'm sorry, I didn't hear."

"They found a gun," she said. "The murder weapon. Police tell me it's the same gun that killed my husband and shot up this photographer; what's his name?"

"Cole Walker."

"They're doing ballistics checks right now. And you can't help me with even a scrap of evidence."

"Why would Eric Lopell kill your husband?"

"Lopell didn't act alone. He had to have help."

A muffle of thunder echoed against the window. Parkin stepped closer to the door.

"I want Lopell's accomplice standing before me in court, tried and convicted. That's what I want. And if you can't do anything more, I'll hire a private detective. I'll do anything until I see someone on death row."

"And what about your husband's possible role in this scam?"

"It was just another job. He didn't know anything."

"Did he talk to you about it?"

She ignored my question. "All I have left are the flowers he sent me. And you, Mr. Bowens, are wasting time."

She opened the door to a torrent. Rain drops the size of dimes flattened as they hit the ground. The sidewalks were washed down and water gushed into the street, pooling where a collection of black olive leaves blocked the drain. Amelia Parkin had an umbrella at her side. She looked at the gray stew of a sky and unsnapped the catch on the umbrella. For several moments, she stood there in the doorway, taking in the cool air. Then she snapped the umbrella closed and held again it to her side. She walked into the rain unprotected, letting the drops cascade down her hair and shoulders. She left the door open and, halfway to her car, she turned and stopped. She stood rigid as a post. Her face was awash in rain, droplets pelting her cheek and forehead. Seconds passed and streams of water rolled down her face seeping into the already drenched blouse. Through the downpour, her eyes kept a firm lock on me. She never blinked. Her glare cut through the slants of rain until I finally closed the door.

Chapter 47

I left three messages on Patrick O'Donnell's phone before I paged him. When he didn't call, Mike Brendon
agreed I should just wait him out. I sat outside the police
building with Ike, but every ten minutes, I alerted the
front desk to try and get his attention for an interview.

He finally arrived forty minutes later. "I know what
you're here for." O'Donnell's 'fro was recently cut, and he
was still brushing hair from his lapels.

"I'm here because of what Amelia Parkin told me."

"I understand that and I had to run information by the
chief to see what we can release."

"And?"

"I think I can address most of what you're going to
ask me."

O'Donnell pulled a legal pad from under his arm. His
ebony fingers scanned down the page until he stopped.
"Before I say anything on camera, can I ask what she
told you?"

"As long as I can get a confirmation on this, yes, I can

tell you that she says you found a gun at Eric Lopell's home. And that the gun is being checked right now."

O'Donnell's expression never changed. "Anything else?"

"I want to advance this story. If Lopell is the shooter in Cole Walker's case, I'd like to report that."

O'Donnell slid the legal pad back under his arm. "Okay, let's do this."

Ike raised the lens at O'Donnell's face, focused the lens, and waited.

"Did you recover a gun at the home of Eric Lopell?"

"We spent all day there and part of the next day, and yes, we recovered a weapon from that home. Right now, the weapon is undergoing a check to see if it was involved in any of the crimes we are investigating."

"Is Lopell a named suspect in the death of Grant Parkin?"

"We can't say anything on that right now. As in any open case, we are looking at everyone."

I asked several more questions involving the death of Lopell, the missing diamonds, and the federal scam probe. All of them were met with police jargon. When Ike lowered his camera, O'Donnell sounded normal again. "Ike, here's the deal. If you know Amelia Parkin, then you know she is pushing hard to slam someone on this."

O'Donnell rolled up the legal pad into the shape of a baton, then he smacked the side of his leg. "We have to give her some facts about the case. Not a lot, but some facts." He hit his leg again. "And sometimes that's not enough. It's hard for a family member to sit at home and do nothing while we scrape the streets looking for a shooter."

"And in this case, the shooter may be dead."

"We'll see," O'Donnell said.

"And when will you get some results back on the gun?"

"Maybe tomorrow."

Chapter 48

Instead of a quick lunch of cramming down a meal and heading off to an interview, Mike Brendon gave me a break from the office. I used the time to visit Cat. Brendon shared my concern about the thug in the fast car.

Dry indentations on the grounds of G.G.'s Garden were now filled with pools of black-tinted water. The leaves of a giant elephant ear were covered with beads of rain drops. I saw Cat a few yards off, resetting plants knocked over by the rainstorm. My sloshing must have alerted Cat and she turned toward me as I approached.

"A daytime visit from Matt Bowens," she smiled. "You here to help me pick up after that storm?"

"Just passing through."

"This far from the office? Why—is there a story out here?"

My smile matched hers. Her face turned serious. "You're worried about me."

"Look Cat. I don't know—"

"Look yourself. We're fine out here."

"It's just this thing is starting to form into a big ugly mess. And I want to make sure you and G.G. are taking precautions."

"By this thing, I guess you mean the murder investigation?"

"I do."

Cat walked past me, her hazel eyes taking on the temperament of a controlled fire. "We're fine," she said.

"All I'm trying to do is—"

"Please, Matt, we're okay," she said turning. I was talking to her back. We walked another twenty feet. Cat sort of marched, while I sidestepped puddles until I finally gave up and let the groundwater soak through my loafers. She stopped inside the shop office where customers paid for plants. I just wanted to pull her close to me. Cat wiped her forehead.

"Listen to me very closely, Matt." She held her hands up, emphasizing each word. "At first, I thought what we both needed right now was space."

"That's not why I've come here."

"I know your intentions are fine. But I've been thinking about this for a long time. And all the way driving back from our trip." She let out a sigh.

"Just the other day we made a promise to talk about this over dinner."

"Maybe it can't wait."

A customer approached, a woman holding a small rubber tree. She saw our faces and backed off.

"I've got to help G.G. run the shop."

"All I wanted to do is come out here, say hello, and show you that I care about you. That's all."

She started to turn, then stopped. "I've been thinking about this. I have to compromise and learn to share you with your job."

I stepped closer. "Give it some time, Cat. I'm trying to save this, not end it."

She paused. "I won't argue about missed trips again. We can work this out." Cat looked in the direction of the customer with the plant, then back at me. The smile returned. "I've got to get back. See ya, Matt."

When I reached the office, Mike Brendon was again searching for video shots from the rooftop camera. A look into the television monitor showed tight close-ups of people on boats. Brendon worked the joystick and zoom controls, focusing on the name of a boat, then pulling out to reveal its crew.

"Not too many boats out today," he said. "Weather's been too bad."

The radio scanners were turned up, probably so he could work the camera and still listen to police chatter and the telephones.

"I got some word back on my tests." Brendon smoothed the top of his hair back into place.

"And?"

"I'm okay. The tests were fine. No diabetes." He paused. "I shouldn't say fine. They were passing. Just barely passing on the sugar levels."

"So what does that mean for you?"

"I've got to watch what I eat. But you know how hard that is?"

"Where's Ike?"

"I sent him to get some shots of a house fire. No one injured, but the house is a total loss."

"You're spending a lot of time with that thing."

"I know. I keep taking manual control away from Miami so I can scan the water. This is great." Brendon had zoomed into a buoy and pulled out.

For the next hour, I sized up my story elements and wrote a script to include the morning the new information on the gun found at Eric Lopell's house, the interviews with Dobb and O'Donnell, and the taped conversation with Campton's secretary.

Ike arrived in time to edit the package. We fed the story by microwave to Miami. Mike Brendon turned up the volume to the bank of televisions on the wall. My taped piece ran four minutes into the newscast. But what caught our attention was the report by Sandra Capers.

She was live outside Eric Lopell's home. After a thirty-second intro, her taped segment started with video of the gun being brought out of the house by a crime tech. The probable murder weapon.

She had the money shot. I didn't.

Brendon stroked his beard. "Looks like Capers got you."

That evening, I spent an hour talking to Cat on the phone. The conversation was split between my visit to the nursery, our dinner dates, and listening to stories about Jason's missing homework or Shauna's latest run-in with a girl in class. As a single man without the experience of raising children, I offered what I could. When I got off the phone, I decided to work out and drove to the basketball court.

The place was lit up with lights, and I was alone to go through my shooting routine. I started with an easy pace and let the problems within me come out through the sweat. Maybe Amelia Parkin was right and I wasn't working hard enough. I let Sandra Capers beat me on a story. But in the cadence of stories I can be beaten one day and soar to an exclusive the next.

When I was shot as a teen, I never thought I'd play again. The court was my solace and I needed the place. I cross dribbled, made a spin move and arched one from thirty-five feet away. For the moment, I tossed my demons into the night sky.

Chapter 50

I almost balked at meeting Adrian Moxer for breakfast. The Perch Walk had a different crowd than the evening group of bikers and beer drinkers. Moxer stared at me the entire time I walked the arrangement of wood planks. The close friend of Eric Lopell started in on me before I had a chance to sit down.

"I heard the stuff you're saying about Eric." He looked as if night time came and went and he forgot to get any sleep.

"Before you get too down on me, I just reported what police told me, that's all."

"Well, they're next on my list. You guys have him convicted, and since he's dead, he can't even defend himself."

"Whether or not he was involved with murder—"

"He wasn't," he bellowed. A waitress heard him and moved in my direction.

"You want anything?" she asked.

"In a minute, I haven't looked at the menu."

"Give him a bowl of snake tongues." Moxer said.

"Two eggs, scrambled, white toast and a few slices of cantaloupe," I told her. "And a cup of coffee." She tucked the menu into a metal holder and tapped a computer screen. "A number two, with 'loupe on the side," she said.

Moxer grabbed a bottle of hot sauce and daubed a piece of toast until the bread looked like it was bleeding. "I didn't think you'd come."

"I never pass on an invitation if it will help the story."

"Now, see, that's where we differ." He tore the slice of bread in half, rolled one piece into a ball of dripping sauce and pushed the mass into his mouth. "Eric wasn't a story. He was a person."

"Eric is part of a much larger story. And you can disagree if you want, but he was also part of a scam to rip off more than a million dollars. And one big question is did he tell you about the rip-off?"

Moxer scratched a faded tattoo on his arm. It took a few seconds to recognize the shape. The tattoo was a knife, just like the one on Lopell's arm.

"Were you a part of Lopell's building climbing days?"

"If I answered that the wrong way to the wrong person, I could be spending a lot of years behind bars eating baloney sandwiches on Thanksgiving."

"Let me phrase that another way. Did you know Lopell back then?"

"To that, I can safely say yes." Moxer pulled the remaining half slice from his plate, emptied the bottle of hot sauce on the bread, and reached for a fresh bottle. "How did you guess?" he asked me.

"The tattoo on your arm. Some kind of gang?"

"Ex-gang. I tried to get the thing removed." He patted his arm. "That's how far back I go with Eric. I played football in high school and he was in gymnastics. I guess his skills came in handy later for his line of work."

"Diamond thefts?"

"What do they say . . . it's only stealing when you get caught."

"But not you?"

"You might say I didn't have the right skills for that."

The waitress placed the plate in front of me, walked down the counter, and grabbed the salt and pepper shakers. "If you need anything else just call."

I was prepared to let my eggs grow cold to get answers. "If you want to help Eric, then answer a few questions." I studied Moxer. He could keep shoving food down his mouth or give up the details to fill in some holes. He ran his hand across the top of his head and stopped when he reached his ponytail.

"Eric wasn't the violent type. Or at least he wasn't before . . ."

"Before?"

"Well, before he ran into this guy. And before you get all intense, I don't know who this guy is. But Eric wasn't approachable anymore."

I took a sip of my coffee. "But Eric let this guy use his car?"

"The Porsche? Yes. He must have sold Eric on the diamond scheme. And with Eric's background, they needed his input. Eric's been scamming all his life."

"Where do you think Eric met up with him?"

"Who knows, the gym, a few night spots. I don't know."

"What about the deal itself? Are you sure Eric never told you about the scam? Try to cut you in?"

"For the record, no. But in time, things were different. Like everything was a big secret."

"And in that whole time, when you were in a gang,

and during the worst of it all, where did Campton fit in to all this?"

"Who?"

For the next five minutes I explained the background of Roland Campton, the warehouse owner, identity thief, and investigation target. Moxer said the name didn't register, but I watched his face and read deceit.

"My people are still looking for Eric's killer," he said.

"The ones at the table the other day. They all have the same tattoo?"

"We couldn't put them on in high school. But after I turned eighteen, we all got them."

Chapter 50

Ike sat off to one side of the police station lobby. I followed O'Donnell outside. "Here's the deal," he started. "We've been talking regularly with Cole Walker by phone. He's been playing this game of calling and not committing to an interview. But he provided some details of what he was hired to do. And then . . ."

O'Donnell's glance turned to the ground then back at me.

"What's the problem?"

"Walker was all set to come in and give us a formal statement and there was even talk of him getting into a sort of witness protection program."

"For Cole?"

"Well, I said sort of protection. We don't have the funds or the means to do that. But the federal government does. We got in touch with them and plugged Cole into their network of protection. But in the last twelve hours, Cole has missed two scheduled rendezvous spots."

"Have you heard from him since?"

"Nothing. He has all of our cell phones, and he always

233

called on other occasions at the precise time. But now that it's time to go into protection, he's a no-show."

I sensed O'Donnell studying me. I thought about Morgan and the still-recovering Cole. "This doesn't sound good."

"I don't want to send out any alarms, but this is where you come in."

"What are you thinking?"

"Matt, we need him to come in. We just thought that one, if you hear from him, please let him know the offer is still out there. He can come forward and the feds would protect him."

"And two?"

"We can't do anything for him unless he comes to us. Now if you want me to say something like that on camera, I will. I want him in here."

I stared at the great expanse of Fort Lauderdale with its combination of older homes and new condominiums rising out of the Federal Highway street noise. And somewhere in that mix were Cole and Morgan.

I got Ike's attention and we did an interview with O'-Donnell saying he wanted to get in contact with Cole. If he saw the interview, Cole would know what was being asked of him.

On camera, O'Donnell talked about the need to find Cole Walker. I changed the subject from Cole to weapons. I asked, "What is the outcome of the ballistics check?"

O'Donnell's brow lines bent downward. He paused. Then he said, "We have finished our initial check of the weapon found during the warrant search and we have determined that it is the same gun used in two, possibly three separate incidents."

"Three? You mean the shooting of Grant Parkin and Eric Lopell. And the third?"

"Without getting into a lot of details, we think the same weapon was used to shoot Cole Walker."

"Any suspects you want to put before the public?"

"Not at this time."

"Are you ready to say at this time that Eric Lopell killed Parkin or shot Cole Walker?"

"We can't make that statement just yet. There's a number of things we are still checking."

We finished the interview and drove to back to the office. I kept stacking up the facts in my mind. The gun in question moved around a lot, from the warehouse and an encounter with Cole, to the hotel and the meeting with Grant Parkin. I pushed it all to the back of my mind and concentrated on the missing man.

Since I had new information on the weapon and the plea for Cole, I did a short story for the noon newscast, using a sound clip of O'Donnell. Near the end of the story, I repeated that the gun found in Lopell's home was the same one used in his murder as well as the death of Grant Parkin.

Chapter 51

In the early afternoon, Mike Brendon heard it first. The police chatter on the scanner was louder. Something garbled. Brendon wrote a few lines on a pad. "I think you and Ike better head toward Federal Highway."

"What are they working?" I asked.

"I'm not sure yet, but it sounds like they found a car."

I moved closer to the scanners. We heard police officers calling to each other from car radios. By the description, it sounded like Morgan's car. Cross streets were given. Ike was already out the door, keys in hand, heading for the news van. I followed him.

It took us just minutes to drive to 9th street. Tucked in next to an ixora bush, I recognized Morgan's car. Two uniforms were standing next to it and one officer was pulling yellow crime scene tape out of his police car. We stopped. Ike ran for his gear. I walked the short distance to Morgan's car until a female cop put her hands up, then pointed at my feet. "The crime tape is going up right there," she said, a soft way of telling me not to move another inch.

"Where's the driver?" I asked.

"Patrick O'Donnell will be here in a few minutes." After holding me in check, she helped the other uniform string more yellow tape across a lawn.

The car was in a driveway, but the angle was all wrong, as if Morgan had to pull over in a hurry. Both car doors were open. On the passenger side of the car, there were three drops of blood on the door. No sign of Morgan or Cole. Ike was in place with tripod and camera, photographing everything. The car, the police, and the house behind the car. After several minutes, Ike looked up from the lens. "Looks like some kind of struggle." He glanced around the street. "I don't see any signs of another car, but someone was here."

I saw the uniforms questioning two people by a police car. Ike followed my stare along the row of houses and unhooked his camera from the tripod. He handed me the microphone, and I stepped off in the direction of people now gathering. The first six people I spoke with didn't see or hear anything. Another four spoke of screeching tires, but saw nothing.

We managed to get two decent interviews before I noticed a police unit driving up and parking near our van. Patrick O'Donnell got out, holding his customary legal pad. He waved us over.

O'Donnell told us, "This is definitely the car belonging to Morgan Walker. If you want an interview, I can give you a few details, but we're still working the scene."

As he finished his sentence Sandra Capers arrived, along with two other camera crews. We all surrounded O'Donnell in a horseshoe arrangement of reporters and cameras.

O'Donnell said, "Approximately thirty minutes ago, we got a phone call from 911." He glanced at his legal pad. "The witness, a driver on his cell phone, said a car was being forced off the road by another driver. At first, the witness thought it was a case of road rage, but the other driver pulled out a gun and forced a man and a woman into his car and they drove off. The male attacker struck the victim with his gun and the car headed south on Federal Highway."

O'Donnell let his eyes drift over the collection of police cars and detectives. "We are working this scene but time is a very real concern for us. The suspect's car is described as a gray panel van. We don't have a license plate, but there was a dent on driver's side of the van."

Then I asked, "Didn't Morgan and her husband miss a date with federal authorities?"

The officer didn't hesitate in saying yes. His answer led to several more questions about Cole, his shooting, and tying it all in to Grant Parkin and Eric Lopell. I turned to Ike. "Cole and Morgan may not have much time."

After seven minutes of questions, O'Donnell backed away from the throng of reporters. I pulled out my cell phone, called Mike Brendon, and gave him as many details as possible. A live truck was on the way, and as soon as a microwave signal was established, I would do a live cut-in.

Truck operator Hank Fullman pulled in next to our news van. He rolled out cable, while the motorized metal mast pumped its way upward, extending some forty-five feet in the air.

"So what do you think?," Ike asked.

I looked at Morgan's car. "It was planned well. Probably one or two cars. Someone bumped into Morgan's bumper." I pointed to the broken taillight. "That bump got her to slow down for a moment. And if a gun was pointed at them, they had no choice but to get into someone's car. But if we don't move fast to find them . . ."

Other live trucks arrived and positioned near Morgan's car. My cell phone thumped a vibration against my side.

"Hello?"

"I'm sorry to bother you, Matt." I heard tones of worry in Cat's voice.

"No bother. What's up?"

"It's just that, G.G. saw that car."

"The Porsche?"

"Yes. It was the same guy who came before to buy the plants."

"Where is the car now?" I heard myself yelling into the phone.

"I don't know. This happened at least an hour ago. Maybe two."

"And you're just now telling me?"

"Don't be upset. I didn't see the car, G.G. did. She didn't think it was a big deal until I told her what you said and I called you immediately."

"What did he do?"

"Well, G.G. said he drove real slow like he was going to pull in, and then he just sat there in the car, staring at the front gate. Then he left."

"Where are you now, still there?"

"Yes. We're fine. I called the police and they sent a car by to cruise the area but they didn't find anyone."

"Cat, why don't you go home for the day?"

"Matt, he's not going to scare me off. The police have

been going past here on a regular basis and we're staying open."

I didn't argue with her. Cat was going to stay put no matter what I said. "Please, be careful." I told her about the discovery of Morgan's car.

I said good-bye and pushed end on my cell phone as Hank Fullman gave me the nod that the signal was in place and Miami could see us once Ike hooked up his camera. By microwave, we fed a portion of O'Donnell's interview, then I stood in front of Ike's camera. I plugged in my earpiece and heard a producer. Her voice sounded as if she was standing in front of me, instead of twenty-five miles to the south in a Miami control room.

"Hiya, Matt," she said.

"We're ready."

I glanced at the small television resting on the ground in front of me. I heard the jingle music in my ear, and the special report animation flashed across the screen.

"Five seconds, Matt," she said.

A voice told a south Florida television audience Matt Bowens was reporting. My face appeared on the television.

"At this hour, a search is on for two people," I started. "From what police tell us Cole and Morgan Walker were in this car." I pointed to Morgan's car across the street. Ike panned the camera over to the spot. "A week ago Cole Walker was found shot over in a warehouse. And since then he has been one figure in a series of events including a murder victim found in his car, missing diamonds, and the recent murder of a man convicted of stealing jewels a few years ago."

Ike panned away from the car and aimed toward the arrangement of cops.

"Police have roped off the car with crime-scene tape and they are talking to witnesses. They are very concerned that the couple have been abducted. At this hour, authorities are looking for a gray van."

I stopped talking. The pause was a signal to Miami to roll the interview of O'Donnell. I watched the screen and saw O'Donnell's face. When he was finished talking, I again saw myself on the TV monitor and I wrapped up the report with the telephone number to Suspect Watch, and said we were now returning to regular programming.

"Thanks, Matt. You're clear." The words came from the voice in my earpiece.

Hank Fullman rolled up the cable and pushed a button allowing the tall metal mast to come down.

"Do we wait here?" Ike asked.

"At least for a few minutes. We don't have another location."

A crime-scene van arrived and two techs got out and checked Morgan's car. A few minutes later, one tech retrieved a small bag and started the task of dusting for prints. Ike zoomed in with his camera and recorded the moment.

Sandra Capers stepped from a group of potential witnesses. Her photographer reached into the top of his camera and removed the tape and replaced it with a fresh one. While I waited for any new word from O'Donnell, I also wanted to interview as many witnesses as possible.

All that changed in the next few seconds.

I heard the hard thunk of a bullet piercing the rear trunk of Morgan's car. The shot was somewhat muffled, but the shot tore a nice hole in the car, raising a small puff of a dust cloud from the faded paint. Both crime techs dropped to the ground, their eyes trained upward on the direction of the shot. I heard screams and saw people running in different directions, all away from the car. Ike was recording the scene unfolding in the street.

It seemed the bullet came from above us. Three uniforms, all in a firm weaver grip, pointed their guns upward, aimed at the arrangement of hotels. They dropped down behind the cars for protection. Another uniform was yelling for people to get back inside their homes. A line of homeowners stood there, in the open, staring up at the multicolored buildings.

The uniforms aimed upward, but shooting wasn't an option. There was no visible target. And the chance of hitting an innocent bystander was probably too great. Hank Fullman was busy inside the live truck. I saw him working controls, as if to reestablish the microwave signal without raising the mast again. Any movement now might make himself a target. I leaned against a tree near the truck for cover.

"You see where the shot came from?" I yelled to Fullman.

He shook his head.

"Any chance of getting us back on the air?"

"Unless I raise the mast, we can't do anything yet," he said. "I'm calling Miami. Maybe they can still see my signal."

Ike stood in the shadow of a huge live oak tree. Maybe, just maybe, he was out of view to the shooter.

Another shot. This time, the bullet smashed the front car window about twenty feet from us. The crash of the windshield sounded like a small explosion. The glass shattered into hundreds of tiny pieces. I heard screams.

The uniforms ran in the direction of the car, all the time keeping their guns pointed upward. When they reached the Honda, two uniforms kept aiming, while a third checked the car for victims. He shook his head and immediately ran back for cover next to the corner of a home. I glanced up.

Each hotel had several stories of parking, starting at the ground and going up. A shooter could be on any of the floors, high-powered rifle in hand, eyes peering through a scope, aiming at the next target. Uniforms had to move fast. I saw them shouting orders into radios and imagined their task was difficult on several levels. They were probably establishing a perimeter around the hotel to get SWAT in place to do a floor to floor check. Homeowners on the street had to stay inside.

I pulled out my cell phone and dialed Brendon. I whispered into the phone. "We're getting shot at . . ."

Brendon shouted back at me, "The police scanners are blasting about it. We're trying to move three more crews to you, but it's not safe just yet."

I checked the live truck. "We can't get a signal."

"Don't worry. We've got the rooftop camera getting some shots . . ." I heard Brendon talking on another phone, then he came back on. "Listen, Matt. Hold on. We're going to patch your phone down to Miami. They can at least hear you. Is that clear?"

"Yes. We'll use the rooftop camera for our video and I'll use my cell as a microphone. I can use the TV here in the truck to describe what's going on."

"Fine, Matt. That's what we'll do. Just hold on. I'm connecting you to Miami."

"Give me a second. I'm a few yards from the truck."

"No problem."

The live truck was no more than several steps away. Before I moved, I made mental checks of what I was about to say on the air. I saw Ike many yards away from me, his camera aimed at police and people running to homes. Uniforms were looking upward, away from my location. A hand wrestled the cell phone out of my grip and tossed it into a nearby yard. I twisted my head to see who was behind me, but a hard nudge of something metal jabbed me in the back.

"Don't turn around, Bowens." The voice was familiar.

I glanced down to catch the glint of a pinky ring and fat fingers holding onto a gun.

His words were aimed at my left ear, "I said don't turn around." The gun was again pushed into my back. "This is one deadline you're not going to make."

Chapter 52

I felt a hand grab my left arm, and Roland Campton stepped me backward, away from the live truck.

"You can let me go and it's probably only assault."

"Shut up, Bowens." His voice was low and even.

He turned me around and an olive green car was parked with a rear door open. I glanced around for help. All eyes were on the hotels.

"Get in." Campton gave me a soft push, and I rolled into the cushion of the back seat. Campton slid in next to me.

"Welcome. You've been invited to the party." The words came from the driver. "I hear you've been looking for me?" He turned his attention away from the street and locked his eyes on mine. "I think we ought to shoot him right here."

His face was an even shade of brown. The smirk of a smile inched toward just one side of his face. His eyes were black darts.

"Where's your Porsche?" I returned his glare.

He said, "Go ahead, shoot him. If you don't, I will."

His face remained transfixed, oblivious to the gathering of police down the street.

"You know that's not the deal," Campton told him. "Let's go."

The face turned around and he put the transmission in drive.

"We've got plans for you." Campton moved the gun so the barrel was aimed at my midsection just below the heart. We eased past a line of arriving police cars. Blue flashing lights reflected off the windows of a furniture store. In less than twenty seconds we were away from it all. Away from Hank Fullman and Ike. Away from being in control of everything around me.

"You don't ask the questions anymore." Campton raised the gun up slightly, pushing the barrel up tight against my sternum.

I was filled with mixed emotions. The rear door was probably locked, but I could wrestle away from Campton and either take the gun or get the door open. I didn't like the odds, but he was right about seeing this through. Perhaps a reporter's curiosity pulled at me. "Were you at the warehouse when Cole got shot?"

"Don't tell him anything," Campton's voice boomed inside the car.

"Let's get this straight, big man. You don't tell me what to do." There was a certain defiance in the driver's voice toward Campton.

I took a chance. "Where's Cole and Morgan?"

All I heard was laughter coming from the man behind the wheel. Ebony fingers grabbed the wheel and he turned east on 17th Street Causeway, heading toward the ocean. Brendon was probably pulling out his beard trying to find me. I should have been on the air by now, broadcasting from the scene of a shooting. Instead, I was moving at gunpoint to an uncertain ending.

"Where are we going?" I said to no one in particular.

Silence.

"You don't think the world will be looking for me?"

Finally Campton said, "Look, if you don't shut up, we're gonna deal with you a bit earlier than planned."

For the next ten minutes, I said nothing. The landscape eased past us. We moved up the bridge spanning the heart of the waterway. On the right, the convention center and Port Everglades. Minutes after leaving the bridge, the driver turned right down a quiet street and pulled around the back of a house. The yard was lined with palm trees and the car stopped at a boat harbored at a private dock.

"Okay, move it." Campton waved the gun and gestured to the door and the boat. When I didn't move fast enough, he jabbed the gun in my back. "You don't want this thing to go off because you didn't move fast enough, do you?"

I got out of the car. Off to my left, there was the yellow Porsche. A row of plants, still in their pots were pushed up against the glass pane of the sliding glass door of the house. I remembered the conversation with Cat about loading them into the car. I searched past the palm trees for a neighbor, or a witness.

Nothing.

"Be my guest." Campton cocked his head in the direction of the boat and a gangplank. I stepped the few feet across the wooden walkway and stepped down into the boat. It was at least forty feet long. Immaculate. A bank of gauges lined a panel behind a steering wheel. A blue Bimini top protected the person at the wheel from the sun.

"Sorry, no tour today. Down!" The driver pointed to the hold of the boat. I took each step down, in slow motion, gauging my way, looking for a way out. A chance of escape. I felt a hard shove into my back and I missed the last few steps, falling hard to the floor. I felt myself slide until I was stopped by someone's legs. I dragged my hand against my mouth. No bleeding. I looked up into the faces of Morgan and Cole Walker.

"Your friend is here," the driver said. His words were matter of fact. "Now we can complete our business." He held a rifle, with scope to his side.

A smile ripped across Campton's face. "Quite a distraction, huh?" Campton took the rifle from the driver's hand and held it up near the ceiling. "He can pop off two shots and get downstairs before any cops get their act together. They stay busy looking for a sniper who is long gone." Campton laughed and handed the rifle back to the driver who walked closer to me until the barrel was an inch from my face. I smelled burned powder and gun oil. He stood there until I turned my head away.

"It's just a warm-up my friend. No TV camera this time." Campton watched over me, the gun pointed at my head, while the driver put down the rifle and wrapped my arms and hands with duct tape. Then he took a long stretch of the tape and wrapped my ankles together. The two of them, Campton and the driver, went back up the stairs. The driver snatched up the rifle as he left. Two sets of soft thuds marked their steps across the boat.

"Sorry about this." Cole Walker would only glance at the floor, his stare failing to move in my direction.

"We don't have much time," I whispered. "Who is the driver, and what are we doing here?"

"His name is Crunon Jackson. They call him Cru. He's the one who shot me."

Morgan's eyes were small beads. She looked like sleep was an option she had avoided for several days.

"What happened, Cole? I mean, I know about the investment scam, but how are you mixed up in all of this?"

He kept staring at the floor, never raising his gaze. Silent and frozen. I raised my ankles and legs and kicked him as hard as I could. His body shifted from the jolt.

"I thought I had this all figured out," he started. "But I was wrong."

"Why am I here, Cole?"

"They think I told you everything. The diamonds, where they stashed the money, everything."

"Everything I learned came from the victims and you. Didn't you tell them I don't know as much as they think?"

"It doesn't matter. They're about to leave the country and now they're tying up loose ends."

"How does Jackson figure in all of this?"

"When they figured out I was against the scam, Cru and Lopell was hired to get me to tell them what I knew. And Lopell was there because of his background with diamonds."

"Why are you telling him all of this?" The scorn was evident on Morgan's face.

"I'm through trying to run from the truth." Cole Walker finally stared at me. I didn't notice at first, but the left side of his face was bruised.

"Lopell?" I expanded my arms, then eased the pressure, testing the duct tape wrappings for any signs of weakness.

"You already know part of it. I've known Lopell for a

long time, going back to his trials." Cole's neck and head sagged back against the wall. "They needed Lopell because he was so good at spewing lies. They needed that kind of input to lure in the investors. But Lopell was a known thug, so he worked behind the scenes. Until . . ."

"Let me guess; Lopell wanted out."

Cole said, "Yes. And there was no way they were going to let him walk the street, knowing the details of a multi-million dollar diamond scam. He had knowledge of everything. So they took him out."

"Who shot Eric Lopell?"

Cole's stare again moved to the floor.

There was a shift up top, and the boat dipped for a moment. A third person was on board. I held out my hand to keep Cole and Morgan quiet. All I heard were muffles, but there was a fresh voice. The visitor walked across the deck, finally stopping where I figured Campton and Jackson were standing. I couldn't make out the words.

"Who is that?" I asked Cole.

He shrugged his shoulders. Finally, "We all answered to a top person. That must be him."

"And this person is?"

"I don't know. I never met him. I always answered to Campton and Lopell. But there was person above them." Cole paused.

"We've got just a few minutes before they come back down here. After that, we may not have any time. Can you get your hands free?"

Cole moved his hands behind him. Morgan struggled against the duct tape. "I think," she said, "I can move my fingers." I heard a ripping sound as she moved her arm forward, stretching the tape until she wriggled her hand free.

"Can you help us with our wraps?"

Morgan bent over and tussled with the tape around Cole's hands. She pulled, then tried to rip the long length. Above I heard the muffled conversation of three voices. I leaned to hear them, then finally I scooted across the floor in a crab walk until I was closer to the stairs. After a few moments, there was movement across the deck. Morgan stopped working on Cole. I stayed in position, determined to hear something. There was a slight dip in the level of the boat and the third person walked off and I heard the soft taps of steps on the gangplank.

I didn't know for certain, but I played with the knowledge that I somehow knew the visitor. I stretched and maneuvered back to my position. Morgan went back to her spot, acting as if she was still firmly tied up.

"There's one other thing," Cole said.

I sat in my original spot and studied Cole's face. "What is it?"

Morgan waited for any movement above, then started in again, trying to free Cole. She stopped and pulled on the tape on her ankles until she was freed.

"They think you have the raw tape," he said.

Raw had one meaning in television. The original version of videotape. "What tape?"

"As a way of protecting myself, one night they thought the camera was off, but I was recording," Cole said.

"Recording what?"

"The whole conversation when they explained the rip-off. How the thing worked, how the money would be divided up. It was long after they thought I was in on the deal. I set up the camera in the back and pretended it was off. They thought I was getting ready to shoot another videotape for their next batch of victims, but before the shoot, I turned on the camera."

"How did they find out?"

"I'm guessing Lopell had suspicions. He recruited me in the first place. I thought I was shooting an in-house infomercial about diamonds. And then I found out people were losing all their money."

"And who told you that?"

"Lopell."

"And Jackson shot you for that?"

"They were trying to get me to come up with the raw tape. Somehow they knew something was on the tape. They thought it was in my car. I don't know how Grant Parkin ended up dead."

"How did he fit into the whole deal?"

"Very little. He was just a courier, paid to deliver flash diamonds. Gems we claimed were made by the diamond-making process. But it was all a lie." Cole paused again. "How Parkin ended up there, I can't figure out."

"And your shooting?"

"A warning. They knew where to shoot me. I was told to give up the tape or else they would go after Morgan. But instead, I lied to them."

"And Lopell was okay with this?"

"Not really. I mean we go way back. I didn't think he'd be involved in beating me. But he was under pressure too. Finally, I gave them a name."

"You told them I had the tape?"

"Exactly. It bought me some time. They didn't believe it for a second, but it saved me."

The puzzle pieces made sense. It explained why they

probably followed me to Cat's nursery. "And you picked up the tape at the warehouse?"

Cole nodded. "The night I was shot, before I went into the warehouse for my so-called meeting with them, I left the tape in the camera and hid it. We had to retrieve it from the garbage bin."

Morgan was still working on Cole's wraps.

"Cole, where is the camera now?"

He stared at me, but refused to answer. We turned in the direction of sounds on the steps. The door opened.

"Are we all getting to know each other again?" Roland Campton let the gun precede him down the stairs. "Go on Cole. Was Mr. reporter there asking you a question? I'm curious as to your answer. What was the question again, Mr. Bowens?"

"It doesn't matter does it?" I said. "You're not going to let us go anyway. So, who was your guest?"

"My, my, Mr. Bowens. Always the one with the quick questions, but never any answers. We're going to have to change that."

I said, "Whatever you think I know, you're wrong. By now, they've got everyone looking for us."

The same grim smile laced across Campton's face. "We've been watching the news upstairs." Campton let out a loud laugh. "Would you believe the SWAT team is still going floor to floor looking for a sniper?"

Campton walked the few steps, stopping by my feet. "Listen, when we fire up the engines, you're going to have a very short time to tell us what we want to know. Where did you hide the videotape?" Campton aimed the gun directly at my forehead.

"You're not going to shoot me right here and bring all that attention to a quiet neighborhood? Put it away."

The gun stayed pointed at me. "Where is it?"

We heard the soft thunder of engines being revved to life beneath us. The boat rumbled with the easy vibration of power ready to be unleashed.

"Hear that?" Campton's pinky ring stuck out from the gun. "We're headed to open water. When we stop again, you'll make the fish very happy."

"Campton." The voice came from Jackson somewhere above deck. "I need your help."

Campton pushed the gun into his pocket and climbed the stairs.

I turned to Cole. "Morgan, keep working the tape. We're in a no wake zone. That gives us less than twenty minutes before moving into deeper water. That's how long we have to do something."

Morgan looked around the room. "There has to be something to cut this stuff."

"Cole," I said. "You never answered my question. "Where did you hide the camera?"

"I'm sorry I got you into this." He kept repeating the same thing over and over. We felt the boat move away from the pier. The engines rumbled and the boat jerked just slightly as the craft was put into gear. The boat moved easily through the water. A no wake zone meant he had to keep the boat going at a slow pace through the marinas.

On each side of the boat were two portals. Each was covered with a drapery. "Morgan, if you can get free and if they leave us alone, maybe you can signal to a ship? Just do something to get their attention," I said.

Morgan shook her head. "But that will take away any time to get your hands free."

"Do what he says," said Cole.

I measured time and distance in my mind and waited.

Chapter 53

I felt the boat move and gray shadows moved across the drapery over the portals. The shapes against the drapes gave me a sense of what we were passing. When we eased past a building, the shadow lasted several seconds. A few minutes later, we passed another boat causing waves to extend our way, so we experienced an up and down movement until the ripples evened out.

"What do you want to do?" Cole couldn't use his hands, so he jammed his face into his shoulder to rub a spot on his nose.

"We only have so much time and then it won't matter. They won't care if they don't have the camera. They'll just dump us at sea and keep going." I looked around the quarters. The place was clean. Nothing on the floor and the walls were bare except for a picture of a Florida sunset made out of tiny mosaic tiles. Anything sharp, which could be used as a weapon or to cut was removed. A small table was bolted to the floor.

"If you get up, check the drawers and shelves," I told Morgan. She rose from the floor and moved as slow as possible to avoid making a sound. Morgan pulled out a drawer. Her eyes scanned the contents and she closed it up and pulled out a second drawer. After reaching her hand inside, she again pushed the drawer closed. Morgan shook her head at us as if the search was futile. She released a clasp on a cabinet door and opened it.

Now I understood what she was finding. The shelves were empty. These guys must be planning on a stop or else they planned to dump the boat, because there were no provisions. They could abandon the boat in the Bahamas, board another, and keep going.

Sunlight then shadow moved across her face. Each cupboard was empty. We were on board with no utensils, no knives, forks, or food. I guessed everything they needed was above deck in another compartment. Morgan pushed the drapery back over one portal, and the sun lit up her face. A constant drone of the engines covered most sounds Morgan would make. But we had to be careful about walking. Sounds coming from the wrong place might mean a visit from Campton.

I followed her stare to her hands. Morgan had removed one of the knobs from a cabinet door, and she pointed the exposed end of a screw at Cole's wrists.

"Nice work," I whispered.

Morgan used the sharp tip to rip at the duct tape. Within a few minutes, his feet and finally his legs were free. Cole angled his hand toward his face and checked the bruise. He got up stiffly as though walking for the first time.

"Thank you," he said.

Both Morgan and Cole inched in my direction. He tore at my bindings. Once freed, we headed for the stairs.

"Let's go," Morgan said. "We can jump overboard and swim."

Cole was about to reach for the handle when the sounds of footsteps grew closer.

The door opened.

"That's enough." Jackson was back at the stairs. A gun was pointed at the three of us. "Did you really think we were going to let you all escape?"

There was a certain edge of confidence in his voice. We missed something. Why would they just let us sit by ourselves, unguarded for so long?

Jackson reached for the roll of duct tape and threw it at Morgan. "Tie him up again."

When she didn't move, he yelled. "Now!"

"You were listening, weren't you?" I told him.

"Every single word." His smile reminded me of someone from my years in the projects.

Jackson made it to me in three quick steps. His right foot filled my chest and he kicked me down. The smile was still there when he came within inches of mc, then gun placed against my temple.

"When we make it to open water, I'm gonna make sure we do you first."

I tried to get a read on what was inside Jackson's heart, but there was nothing. He glanced over at Morgan. Cole was taped up again and he was back in his familiar spot on the floor. Jackson eased the gun away from my temple.

"How did you hear us?" I asked.

His smile returned. "Sure. I'll show you." Jackson glanced over to the mosaic-tiled sunset and took the picture off the wall. A wire was connected to the back of it.

"The microphone is right here." He tapped the gun against a portion on the picture. "The sound is pretty good."

"Did you hear what you wanted?" I said.

"Almost." Jackson put his gun down and taped Morgan. He stared at Cole. "You just about gave us the location of the camera. But that's okay. We'll make one more attempt to get it out of you before . . ."

He never finished.

Jackson turned in my direction. "Mr. C. wants to see you. Without them."

He put the gun in his waist and checked the bindings on Cole and Morgan. I thought about rushing him.

"Nothing funny, mind you, and we'll end this right here," he said.

I rubbed the stickiness off my wrists. The familiar nudge of a gun barrel was again shoved against my back. I went upstairs, feeling Morgan's eyes on me.

I shook the blood back into my legs and by the second stairstep I got my bearings. Once uptop I knew where we were. I glanced at the open part of the waterway and recognized a small office building and residential homes. As we moved away from them, they took on a blur of graying lines of stucco. The air was good. A breeze caught me in the face and I stood there, not moving, facing the back lots of buildings lining the seawall. I was rigid, firm in place, and was prepared to stay there as long as I could, legs locked in position until I had no choice but to move.

"Go!" Jackson held the gun in my back. "Mr. C. is waiting." I felt the metal pushing at me. Jackson held onto my belt. If I tried to jump, I knew my leap into the water would be accompanied with a bullet to the head.

I studied the intracoastal water. There were no boats near us. And the mouth of the cut was close. The inlet was made up of large rocks stacked on top of each other. Once we were through the cut, we'd reach seas of one thousand feet deep in about twenty minutes.

Roland Campton sat in the captain's chair. He looked straight ahead at the few boats lining up to move through the cut.

"This is going be our last time to talk." He kept his eyes forward.

I wanted to force him to look at me, but he kept his face ahead on the water. "What you need to do is turn around and let us go."

"That's not possible. There's too much at stake. But there is something you can do for me." He finally turned in my direction. "I need that information." He flipped a toggle switch on the dashboard, and I heard Morgan and Cole talking to each other. Their voices were coming through a small speaker mounted on the dash. Morgan was scared and Cole tried to reassure her.

"I thought for a minute there he was going to tell you what we need. But this is your last chance." Campton adjusted the sunglasses on his face, the pinky ring reflecting off the black glass.

"If you think he's going to tell me—"

"That's exactly what I think," Campton cut me off. "The videotape is in the camera, and I want it in my possession."

"And if he tells me, then all of a sudden you're going to turn around and set us free?"

Campton didn't respond. "Here's the way it works," he started. "You go back down there and get him talking. He tells you what we want and we'll consider putting you in the water minus the weights." Campton's laugh boomed across the bow.

"Why did you kill Lopell?"

Campton didn't hesitate. "Man got all righteous on us. Didn't want to be involved anymore, he says. Didn't want to rip people off anymore, he says. I told him that's what he's good for. I shot him and Jackson helped me dump the body in the 'glades."

I knew I risked any chance of being freed, but I had to arrange the sequence of events. First, the whole scam was crumbling. Fast. Then Cole decided to become a state witness. Eric Lopell wanted out and died for his troubles.

"How does Grant Parkin fit into all this?"

Campton looked back at Jackson and his laughter was louder than before. "That's one piece you'll never figure out."

I kept pushing. "You took the gun used to kill Lopell and Parkin and stashed it at Lopell's home to make it look like he killed Parkin. But why?"

"You're not operating with all the facts. And when you have that, then maybe you complete the puzzle, but right now I need you to go back down there and find out what Cole knows. Because if I have to step in, it won't be pretty. You got it?"

Jackson cocked his head and led me in the direction of the stairs. I almost made it to the last step when I felt Jackson's foot against my back. The kick sent me crashing against the base of a table leg. I no longer cared about the gun or the man pointing the weapon. Anger took up a place in my heart, boosting my adrenaline and making me focus everything on the man standing over me. I got up swinging, missing his jaw by inches. When I heard the gun being cocked, I stopped.

"Down, now."

I didn't see Jackson's face, his arm, or the hand holding a weapon. I only saw the barrel. I sat down and waited for the duct tape to be thrown at me to begin wrapping my ankles. In a few minutes I was back on the floor, hands and ankles tied. Jackson walked over to me, bent down and put his knee on my chest. He got closer and whispered. "You know I've seen her."

My mind pulsed back to the conversation with Cat about a guy and a Porsche stuffing plants in his car.

Jackson said, "When I'm through dropping you over the side, I'm going back to get her." He let out a small laugh and kept the weight pressed down on my heart. "She's beautiful, you know. I've talked to her up close. Soon, she'll get to know the real me."

I twisted my body to the left, causing his knee to slide off my chest. At least for the moment. Jackson had me pinned down. I coughed into the smooth deck floor. He got up and made his way to the steps.

"Keep talking," he said. "Your conversation is keeping you alive." He left.

For several minutes, I remained in the same position, coughing for air, and waiting for the moment I could face Jackson. I'm not sure how much time went by before the silence was interrupted by a question.

"What did Campton say to you?" Morgan angled her face in my direction.

I glanced at the sunset picture then back to Morgan. "They want to know where the camera is located. And Campton is serious about finding it."

Cole leaned in, keeping his voice low. "Let's just say, the check's in the mail." He smiled.

"What does that mean?"

No answer.

I rested my head back against the wall. The boat picked up speed. We were leaving the no-wake zone. The portals gave us some idea of what was going on outside the vessel. The bow of the boat raised up and the engines were unleashed. Each new wave smacked the bottom of the boat, saltwater sprays hitting the portals. Uptop I knew Jackson and Campton were holding on to deck rails and bracing for each approaching wave as the engines powered the boat through the crests.

Below, we were like spilled marbles. Morgan fell over on her side and the three of us careened around the floor with each thump of a wave against the hull. We were traveling much faster now, moving on to deeper water.

Chapter 54

All conversations ended. Without the use of our hands, all we could do now was somehow use our bodies to grip the floor. We were sliding around. My stomach churned with each rise and fall of the waves and I knew sea sickness would follow if the boat didn't turn back.

I learned to move my body in cadence with the ocean. I lost track of time. Was it ten minutes? Twenty? Cole appeared to be in severe pain. He bled from the beating during the kidnapping, and he was still recovering from the gunshot wound. Morgan rolled over to his side, and together they formed a two-person bond against the turbulence. She held on to him, pressing her body against his, shielding him from bumping into the baseboard.

"My shoulder," he moaned. Cole collapsed his body into a fetal position. It was torture. His gunshot wound probably sent lines of pain through him.

We were tossed around until I heard Campton cut the engines, and the hard pounding stopped. Now we experienced the slow rise and fall of each wave. I felt a gurgle down in the pit of my stomach. Up top, two sets of feet crisscrossed the deck, and the sounds of doors opening and closing echoed down through the hatch.

"They're getting ready for something." Cole's head rested on the floor. He looked defeated. "The check's in the mail." He spoke so soft, I don't think Jackson and Campton heard him. Besides, they were probably too busy to notice. My stare again roamed the galley for anything to be used as a weapon.

Above, the commotion stopped.

Morgan righted herself. "We can't let them do this. Tell them what they want to know." There was anger in her voice. She turned in Cole's direction. "Tell them about the camera."

Cole stayed silent.

I said, "He never told you what he did with it?"

"There was a moment when he took the car and when he came back, the camera was gone. Only he knows where."

There was a heavy foot on the second step. "Show time." Campton eased his girth down the stairs, followed by Jackson, who held the gun.

"We're going to take you up one at a time. Once that's done, we'll prepare you for the drop."

Morgan's hands were untied by Campton. The duct tape came off in ripped strips, which he tossed in a corner. Morgan struggled against Campton's grip on her arm.

He shook her body, the strands of her hair kicked out in all directions. "Forget it," he yelled. Campton held firm to Morgan's arm, pulling her up the steps, then they both disappeared up on deck. Jackson stayed below, keeping the gun pointed at us.

"Next," Campton shouted.

"Let's go." Jackson stepped in my direction. He followed the same routine. The gun went in the back of his waist, then he tore the duct tape away from my hands and ankles. The gun was again pointed at me and he pushed me toward the lowest step. For a moment, Jackson looked at Cole.

"You're last," he said. "We want you to hear what you're missing."

In a few seconds, I joined Morgan. She was sitting in a chair, and Campton was forcing her into a jacket. But I could tell, the jacket was full of something to weigh it down. The material sagged with round circles. Campton smiled at his work.

"A little something to make the trip go faster." He reached into a bag and produced a chain. Every few links or so, a lock was attached to the chain and with the lock, another weight. I was next. Jackson gave the gun to Campton and he pulled another weighted jacket from the bag. He held the thing up and his stare turned to a corner where bags of chum rested on the deck. Stuff used to lure fish.

"First the jacket, then the chum." Jackson came closer with the jacket. "The chum will bring out the big boys. And after we nick you up a bit . . ." Next to the chum was a long bladed knife.

The calm of the wave action was interrupted by something in the air. The noise was mechanical and getting closer by the second.

"Look out!" Campton shouted. "Helicopter."

I recognized the distinctive off-white color as a police helicopter, followed close by the orange-colored chopper from the U.S. Coast Guard. I guessed the choppers would be over us in thirty seconds. I didn't want to wait to see if it tailed away from us. Jackson's attention was still on the helicopters. Campton held the gun at me, but his eyes were focused on the approaching aircraft.

I reached down, channeling my strength into the fingers tightening into a fist, ready to take aim at Jackson. The hard revolutions of helicopter blades were on top of us now and the wind kicked at the boat. My arm came forward, using my fist as a fulcrum to launch a punch at Jackson's face.

He dropped the jacket and reeled backward, jabbing a hand to his chin as if surprised. The helicopter noise was drowning out anything we might have said. Rather than look at the pilot or anyone on board the copters, I moved in on Jackson, picking up the heavy jacket and swinging the thing over my head in big circles.

A voice boomed down from the helicopter through a loudspeaker. "Put down the gun." Campton was still aiming the weapon at the orange craft in the sky. "This is your last warning, put down the gun."

Jackson backed up against the rail and stopped. Campton turned his attention away from the helicopter and started to aim the gun at me. I turned toward Campton and connected with the jacket. The weights caught him flush on the right side of his head, and Campton careened off the side of the boat into the blue-black water. The gun went with him. I looked up and stared into the barrel of a rifle aiming down from the helicopter. Over Jackson's shoulder I saw the familiar flashing blue lights of the marine patrol. Campton yelled for help. He bobbed in the water, waving to the approaching boats. Jackson slumped down to the surface of the deck. His hand propped against the door of a storage bin and it popped open, sending a rifle sliding out onto the deck.

"Don't even try it," I told him.

"Why not? I can go out shooting."

"The second you reach for that rifle, they'll open up on you. Just wait for them to come get us."

Jackson smiled. Through the whirling blades, approaching sirens, and Campton yelling for help, I heard Jackson's whisper.

"Let'm try."

He reached down, slow at first, then snatched up the rifle with a quick grabbing motion. He swirled and aimed upward. A bullet from above whistled over the blue canvass bimini top.

"Put down the gun!" The order came from the helicopter. Jackson turned and now aimed the rifle at me. He didn't even look through the scope. He just leveled the weapon at my stomach.

"Think about it," I said. "You put that down, and you get to tell your side of this to a jury. Who knows, maybe they'll see it your way."

The second shot made us both jump. The bullet smacked into the water, a line of bubbles tracing the hot metal into the dark water. That made two warning shots, but I knew the next one would be aimed at Jackson.

"Cru. Put the rifle down. Do it now."

He stared at me. Three marine patrol boats were now just yards from us, weapons pointed at Jackson from all directions. He eased the rifle down to the deck. He stood, never moving from the spot until the uniforms boarded the boat and cuffed him. Through it all, he didn't take his stare from me. Campton was pulled from the water, and someone gave him a towel before putting him in handcuffs.

Chapter 55

I lost track of the number of police cars waiting for us at the dock. There was an unusual moment watching Ike zoom in on me and photograph my steps on land at the U.S. Coast Guard base in Fort Lauderdale. Sandra Capers was there, microphone in hand, waiting to interview me, Morgan, or Cole.

Campton and Jackson were ferried by police boat to another destination, and eventually, the county jail. If Mike Brendon was sharp, he should have at least another crew already in place at the gate of the jail to photograph their walk from police cruiser to lockup.

Over the next twenty minutes, we took turns in front of a semicircle of cameras and reporters. We thanked the Coast Guard and Marine Patrol. I had a sense of how they found us and all during my time standing on the deck of the boat with a gun in my back, I hoped Brendon was watching the water. Once we finished the interviews, the eyes of Cat Miller cut through the crowd of faces. I ran to her open arms.

"We were worried. Are you okay?" She finally stepped back from me to inspect.

"I'm fine."

Once her hard glance checked me from foot to head, she again thrust her body into mine.

"How did you hear about this?"

"Well, first I got a call from your assignment editor. He said he wanted me to know you were missing before I heard about it on the news."

"And the kids?"

"They're fine. They're with G.G."

Over Cat's shoulder I saw Ike tapping his watch. Channel 14 probably had a long list of duties for me. Cat's smile turned serious as she studied my eyes.

"I can't hold on to you forever." Cat released her hug. "When they're done with you, we'll talk." I pulled her into me one final time, taking in the mixture of her scent. I let her go. Cat walked backward and smiled, keeping a lock on my face until she reached the parking lot.

"Man, you had us worried." Ike Cashing set his camera on the ground and shook my hand. "We got your interview, but the station wants a live interview with you, and they're going to roll some video over your comments. We're set up right over here. You're the story, man."

Live-truck operator Hank Fullman looked down rather than meet my glance.

"What's up? You ready for some live TV?" I told him.

He didn't answer but instead kept rigging the area for the live feed. He draped a microphone over the top of a chair and set up a television. "What's wrong?"

"It's all my fault." Fullman kept his eyes pointed to the ground.

"It's not your fault. There's no fault here. Everyone was distracted by the sniper. It's okay." My voice was loud enough to cause a few heads turing in our direction.

"You were there, and then you disappeared. You couldn't have been more than twenty feet from me. I should have seen something."

"Look, Hank. These guys set this all up to do this right under everyone's nose. They were armed. Even if you saw something you would have been in jeopardy. I'm okay. It's a good thing you didn't get involved."

His glance drifted up from the sand washed ground. "You're all right?"

"Fine. Ready to do some television."

Once in place, I sat down for a fifteen-minute long special report. Two anchors in Miami asked me a list of questions while they ran video of the boat. A Channel 14 helicopter with a camera mounted on the front captured video of Jackson's arrest and Campton being pulled from the water.

Once the interview was finished, I had a brief talk with the station attorney. He would sit in with me when it was time to give a statement to police on what happened. But I still had a number of questions.

"You can thank the rooftop camera." Mike Brendon stood in the video feedroom, admiring his gadgets and joystick mounted on a panel. "This baby got it all."

I stood off to one side, flanked by Ike and a small group of reporters and photographers assigned to the story. "So how did this all work?"

A flash of pride edged each of his words. "You see, I already had the camera up and working. You remember that the rooftop camera was recording video of the neighborhood because of the sniper shots. So we were focusing on that area." Brendon worked the controls. On a TV monitor, we saw a wide shot of the intracoastal.

"I was counting on you to see us," I said.

"When you turned up missing, I didn't know what to think. I used the camera to search everything. I mean, I checked the streets, the spot where they found Morgan's car. I had this thing pointed at rooftops, at the port. Everywhere. And then I found this." Brendon kept the camera trained on a spot in the middle of the waterway. "I don't know why but I started checking boats leaving the intracoastal. I saw something, and I started recording. That's when I saw you."

Brendon hit a play button on a video deck. A tape played. We stood and watched video of me being ushered across the top deck of the boat, with a hand jammed up against my back. "And with these controls . . ." Brendon pointed to the zoom feature on the panel. We watched the picture zoom in close enough to see the dark outline of a gun barrel resting at the square of my back. Cru Jackson's face was clear and defined. Campton still had his face directed away from the camera, but the video was good.

"That's when I called police. They got the patrol boats, the Coast Guard, and the world chasing you down."

"Thank you." I shook his hand. "There was a moment there, when I was being moved at gunpoint where I was up on the deck. I saw the Channel 14 building and I stood there, hoping another boater would spot me. But I had no idea . . ."

"Just so you know," Brendon started. "They found out Campton's real identity. His name is Carson Balter.

Seems he's took the name Campton from a guy in southern Illinois."

The group broke up from around me. We each had an assignment to do. One reporter was given the task of putting together a story on the scam, from beginning to now, using video of the informercial put together by Cole Walker. There were new interviews with victims reacting to the arrests. Another reporter focused on the Walkers, a third did the nuts and bolts of the sniper attack and my rescue. And that left the witness account to me. I glanced at my watch. Three P.M. Our 5:00 news was just hours away, and a nagging concern was still notched in my mind when the phone rang.

"Bowens here."

"I thought you were set to be fish bait." The voice of Frank Tower faded in and out.

"Where are you?"

The cell phone reception wasn't perfect. "I know you've got a lot going on, but if you want to wrap this thing up, you might want to meet me somewhere."

Chapter 56

Five police cars and two crime-tech vans surrounded the house. Ike pulled up next to an unmarked detective car and we got out. There were no reporters in sight. When we drove up and I conjured up the picture in my mind, I knew the identity of the third person on the boat.

Frank Tower stepped out of his SUV, pulling on the bill of his baseball cap. "Welcome. I see you're still in one piece." Tower walked as he spoke. Ike positioned the camera on his shoulder and we kept pace with the quick gait of the insurance investigator. I recognized the algae-stained pond next to the stucco house. And I remembered the pleas in front of cameras asking for help in finding a killer.

I didn't figure it all out on the boat, but the pieces were there: the light step off the boat, and the possible glimpse of hair at the small of a back. Six uniforms were still stretching up rolls of yellow crime tape, but they let Tower go all the way up to the front door. We followed him. He still had friends on the force. The door was open and I saw one person in handcuffs.

Amelia Parkin.

She had her face turned away from us. Crime techs were all through the house, lifting pieces of art or dusting cabinets for prints. One uniform looked at us as though we were trespassing on an investigation. We got the stare to move back.

"They're with me. Is that okay?" Tower waited for an answer. The uniform kept going. "Her friends, Jackson and Campton, didn't waste any time in talking," Tower said. "The units got here just in time. Another five minutes and she would have been gone."

Ike raised his camera at Parkin. There were no objections. "Just don't go inside," Tower warned. "Stay right here by the door."

Then Parkin turned her gaze toward the camera and shouted, "You've got the wrong person. Lopell is guilty."

"Sure he is," Tower cracked back. "Your lie didn't go far."

I pointed the microphone in her direction. "Why?"

Without the use of her hands, she managed to whip the trails of hair away from her face. "My husband was weak. A small-time weakling with no guts. Roland never backed down from anything. Get out of here." Parkin turned her face away from Ike's camera.

"You're looking at the person who came up with the idea for the scam," Tower whispered. "She and Campton were having an affair. But you won't find her on tape talking about it. She's too smart for that. Her husband did all the talking. Right now Campton, her lover, is telling police she set up Lopell. And she stashed the gun in Lopell's home. Campton is confessing to killing Lopell. Jackson shot your friend Cole, and that lady right there, she shot Grant Parkin."

"Her husband?"

"Sure. He wanted to keep the deal small. But she saw megamillions. Let's just say they had a difference of the minds. It was easy to meet up at the Clarkson Hotel. Cru Jackson parked Cole's car in the lot of the hotel. Her husband didn't know anything about shooting Cole at the warehouse. He thought he was going to meet Cole at the car, but good old Amelia had other plans. Parkin got popped, Campton took her home, and then she cried on every TV station in town." Tower looked at me with an uneven smile. "Are you feeling a bit used right now?"

The stories of Ameila Parkin pleading for the public's help were seared into my memory. Ike finished shooting video and was ready to step back.

"Don't leave just yet," Tower instructed. "I'm playing out a hunch." We watched him walk into the foyer and whisper into the ear of a crime tech, then he stepped to the counter, stopping at the ceramic flower vase. The thing was black from finger print powder. Twelve very dead flowers were still standing, rigid and void of any color. The veins in Amelia Parkin's neck raised up. "Leave that alone. That came . . ."

"I know," Tower shouted back. "They came from your husband." He stood in front of the vase but didn't touch it. The crime tech did. Wearing plastic gloves, he lifted the vase and tilted it forward. It appeared there was no water, but I could tell there was still some heft in the vase itself.

"Put it down." Ameilia was shouting now, rising up out of her place on the couch. A uniform took a step toward her, but Tower waved him off.

"That's mine," She screamed. Ike was up and recording.

"What's in there?" Tower asked.

She didn't respond. Her eyes glared through the strands of hair now covering her face. The crime tech was careful not to touch the sides of the vase and instead used his gloved fingers at the top and very bottom of the vase to tip it over. I glanced at Ike who appeared to be zooming in on the vase. The tech was easy with the vase, tilting the top down gently. I heard a rush of things rolling forward in the vase until the tech tipped the top of the vase down.

They came out with a glimmering splash, all coated with watery plant material, yet they hit the kitchen countertop with flashes of glinted sparkle. We stood in awe of the once missing diamonds.

Chapter 57

Two days passed and we all stood in the newsroom as the mail carrier put the package down on my desk. He gave us a curious look before leaving. The package had my name on it, and I was given clearance to open it even though Detective Victor was standing to my right ready to take the contents into possession as soon as the wrapping came off.

"You lied, didn't you?" My question was directed at Cole Walker who stood off to one side, still favoring his shoulder. Morgan was next to him.

Walker said, "I didn't lie. I said, the check was in the mail. It's not a check but close."

I peeled the top of the envelope away. "And it's not a camera. That's just what you told them."

"As a photographer, I would never try to part with my camera, unless it was a real emergency. The camera is in storage. But what you have right here is the videotape I shot of the meeting." Cole started to pick up the tape, then put his hands at his side. "They must have sent Lopell by my house to look for it that night you were with Morgan.

278

He's the one Morgan spotted in the window. They were looking for the tape."

A crime tech moved in and took a picture of the package, which was addressed to me. Once I opened it, the tech took another photograph and Detective Victor stepped in and pulled out a videotape from the envelope with a pen. Once he recognized the tape, he pushed it back into the envelope next to a note. The tech snatched up the prize, placed the package into an evidence bag.

"We don't have the money yet," Detective Victor started, "But we've got a good lead on where they stashed it." He thanked us and left with the tech.

The Channel 14 attorney stood in the back near the edit machines. Before the turnover of evidence, there was a long talk between the attorney, the police, and Cole Walker. In conversations, Cole intended for me to hold on to the tape for safekeeping. Not keep it. The station pondered the situation and agreed the actual ownership of the tape belonged to Cole and not Channel 14. And since Cole planned to give it to police anyway, we followed that wish rather than fight to hold on to it.

"Why didn't you just send it to the police in first place?"

"Maybe I just trust you."

"Good, then you won't mind going on camera."

Cole and Morgan Walker turned in the direction of Ike, who was standing behind his gear. Two chairs were placed in front of Ike.

"We've done some interviews already," Morgan said.

"There are still a few questions," I told them.

Morgan looked at Cole before answering me. "It was me who came to you in the first place. We can sit down for a few minutes."

Cole took up the chair to my left, still favoring his shoulder. Morgan sat next to him. I grabbed a chair and waited for a cue from Ike. He nodded and I raised the microphone toward Cole.

"I know you are cooperating with police, but did you, in any way benefit from this rip-off?"

"No, I did not. Well . . ." He paused.

"Let me explain," Morgan said. "This is hard for both of us, since we didn't want anyone to get hurt. When I first approached you, Matt, I had two rather large diamonds. That was Cole's payment—"

"You don't have to do this," Cole interrupted. "It's my fault I got us into this. They gave me the biggest diamonds I ever saw. That's how they paid me. At first I didn't know if they were real."

Cole tapped his chest with his hand. "This is supposed to be a warning, a reminder. They shot me and called police. These guys didn't want to kill me, just scare me."

Morgan said, "I had to know if those diamonds were real or fake. That's why I had you take me to see the jeweler. I really wasn't sure what was in the tape box."

"After awhile, I didn't want the diamonds," Cole said. "Not if they came from profits of the scam. I just tucked them away."

"And the diamonds are still with the police?" I asked.

"Yes," Cole said. "When they are no longer needed as part of the investigation, we plan to sell them and use all of the money to start repaying the victims."

Morgan's glance was now centered on Cole. "We just want to walk away from this. Testify and move on."

Chapter 58

The Small Guys roller-coaster chugged to a stop and wasn't in a rest position for five seconds when Jason begged to ride again.

"We have to get in line one more time," I explained, but the seven-year old didn't seem to grasp the concept of wait.

The lure of cotton candy, haunted mansion rides, and the merry-go-round played a part in his willingness to move on.

"I can't believe we're here a second time in a month." Shauna kept the pace for us and directed which way we should go.

"Thank you," Cat said. "The kids don't mind coming back."

"No problem. I'm just glad you understand."

"I admit, I didn't at the time. But that's over."

The station gave me a week off to get away and recharge. I parlayed a Monday school day off and used the three days to book a hotel near the amusement park.

Shauna took off running toward the ice-cone machine, followed close by Jason.

"Let's go," Shauna shouted. Cat smiled at me, then broke away in an easy gait to catch up to them. I stepped off to match her stride. I didn't want to get left behind.